BRAND X

The Boyfriend Account

BRAND X
The Boyfriend Account

Laurie Gwen Shapiro

delacorte press

Published by Delacorte Press
an imprint of Random House Children's Books
a division of Random House, Inc.
New York

Delacorte Press and colophon are registered trademarks of Random House, Inc.

www.randomhouse.com/teens

Educators and librarians, for a variety of teaching tools,
visit us at www.randomhouse.com/teachers

Library of Congress Cataloging-in-Publication Data
Shapiro, Laurie Gwen.
Brand X : the boyfriend account / Laurie Gwen Shapiro.—1st ed.
p. cm.
Summary: When she lands an internship at an advertising agency, high school
junior Jordie gets some dubious help from her new colleagues who suggest
that she try advertising techniques to attract a handsome boy at school.
ISBN-13: 978-0-385-73288-8 (hardcover : trade)—
ISBN-13: 978-0-385-90309-7 (hardcover : Gibraltar lib. bdg.)
ISBN-10: 0-385-73288-0 (hardcover : trade)—
ISBN-10: 0-385-90309-X (hardcover : Gibraltar lib. bdg.)
[1. Interpersonal relations—Fiction. 2. Advertising—Fiction.
3. High schools—Fiction. 4. Schools—Fiction.] I. Title.
PZ7 .S295673Br 2006
[Fic]—dc22   2006004596

The text of this book is set in 12-point Goudy.

Printed in the United States of America

October 2006

10 9 8 7 6 5 4 3 2 1

First Edition

This book is for the supremely off-kilter
Mark Newgarden and Jordan Bochanis,
despite the fact that they had me
double-scrub their coffee mugs.

BIG *thanks* **to:**

Beverly Horowitz for her risk-taking, editing, and moral support—and her assistant, Rebecca Gudelis.

My level-headed agents, Nancy Yost and Michael Cende-jas, who always patiently listen to some truly bizarre ideas for novels without snorting—and their assistants, Mercedes Marx and Carlyn Coviello.

Branding guru Douglas Atkins for his time and expertise.

My dear pals (and trusted guinea-pig readers) Corey S. Powell and Joanna Dalin.

My husband (and best friend), Paul O'Leary.

*Imagine a million-dollar
ad campaign all devoted to
rebranding you!*

You, the client, must have an

inkling of exactly who you want.

(Write his name down now.)

To get what you want,

you must know what it is.

Set a goal.

Gorgeous. Smart. Athletic. That's the description of the guy you want. The only problem is that he won't give you a second glance.

But what if you had an ad agency helping you—directing every move of your crush strategy?

That's right. Professional people. The best creative brains out there.

Forget about Nike, Coca-Cola, McDonald's.

I'm talking about a campaign to make *you* the most sought-after hot item around. Or in professional shoptalk, you as a brand.

What you are about to read *actually happened* to me during my junior year of high school. It was only a little while ago that I took part in a "real world" internship program designed to give teens a taste of adult life. It's still hard for me to believe everything that happened.

The rules of the program: I had to keep a diary of what I learned. During my internship the mentors at the ad agency jokingly suggested I should use their creative brains and strategies to get the most desired guy in my class. So I started a much more personal spiral notebook too and just turned in the official one.

So I have two notebooks. Enough time has passed that I'm finally ready to make sense of everything, and I also feel that I can help others make some sense of this crazy process.

Whether you want to sell *yourself as a girlfriend* or sell a can of soda, there are more than a few principles and tips of the trade to benefit from. No kidding. The millions of bucks in the ad world exist for a reason.

1. Wipe the Slate Clean

This is the most important rule of marketing.
Before any big project begins, free the brain.
Go for a walk or run. (It doesn't have to be down
Madison Avenue.) Relax however you do that.
(Don't start e-mailing him mushy notes.)
You're not ready for <u>any</u> action yet.
Relax, and get ready to focus.
Now, focus.

All of a sudden I heard thunder. I ran for 179 Spring Street before the brewing storm hit my few feet of lower Manhattan.

I pushed open the filthy doors and the lobby was not so great. Right next to the scratched elevator was a garbage can that desperately needed to be emptied. My face was still wet with rain as I checked the slip of paper again to be sure I had the right address for the ad agency.

How could this building possibly be where a fancy ad agency was located? My father loves telling our out-of-town relatives on his embarrassingly braggy tours of New York City that the reason so many Manhattan lobbies are grubby is to trick robbers into thinking that there's no plush furniture and pricey electronics upstairs.

The door to suite 3B was held ajar by a glittery rubber stopper, a small thing, but such a funky thing that it gave me hope. On the side of the white door, the words OUT OF THE BOX were stenciled in green. Nobody answered when I knocked, so I let myself in.

How cool was this reception area? The nearest walls were candy-box red and the ones opposite a lemony yellow. Over the unmanned reception desk was an enormous painting of a multicolored lollipop that was actually spinning around because of some unseen mechanism. On the opposite wall above the red velvety couch was a cartoony Dalmatian painting. The two chairs on either side of the couch were upholstered in velvet, the purple of royal capes. Somehow the freaky decor hung together perfectly, like the eye-popping design of the week on one of those strangely addictive cable decorating shows with a bubblehead hostess.

"Hello?" I called out softly and a bit nervously. No answer. I didn't know what to do with myself. I noticed the vintage children's toys on the long glass table in front of the couch. I picked up a red plastic whistle shaped like a fish and put it back down. Maybe if I waited for a minute, the receptionist would come back. I decided that I definitely had the wrong outfit on for this interview. At my school internship coordinator's suggestion, I'd put my beloved jeans aside for the morning and played it safe with a button-down shirt and a pleated black skirt.

"Hello?" I said much louder.

Maybe the entire staff of the ad agency was in an unexpected board meeting and forgot about the high school kid hoping to work there for school credit five half days a week. I peered into a few open offices down the long corridor. If I saw anyone, I'd just nicely remind them that the kid was here, that's all. One room had a long shelf covered with a Pez dispenser collection–there were Snoopy and Bart Simpson and Humpty Dumpty heads crowning those familiar long rectangular Pez bodies. In the same room there was a rack of dress-up hats like in my little cousin's preschool. Except the fireman's hat and the white puffy chef's hat and the princess cone were adult-sized.

The kitchen area, which I found next, was empty too. But the items on a little round table made me laugh. Next to an open tin of orange and black sugar cookies—shaped like ghosts, pumpkins, and witches—was a plastic toddlers' cow barn with a tin roof and rooster weathervane, complete with plastic grain in the attached silo. I snuck myself a ghost cookie. The lights were on in Out of the Box, but someone must have forgotten to turn them off. Someone could have just been playing with the barn—the two pigs were placed right up next to the pig trough.

I grabbed a paper cone from the watercooler. I hadn't had anything to drink since homeroom, when I had my usual carton of pineapple-strawberry-orange juice.

"Well, well, well, looks like we have a visitor."

I almost spat out the water. A short man with a thin, wiry body and one of those hipster goatees (that look like a bit of chin dirt) had mysteriously appeared in the doorway. I crumpled the incriminating paper cup into my skirt pocket and quickly wiped off the sugary white crumbs.

"You must be our internship candidate, yes?"

"Yes," I said softly. At that moment I heard more muted voices from another room.

"We didn't hear you come in. So sorry about that. It's a

staff holiday here, you see. It's the company president's birthday, so my team snuck into his office to see if we could have more ideas sitting in leather chairs."

"You're here even though it's a vacation day?" I'd never actually been on a big interview before. Why did I ask that?

He smiled warmly. "Our lot is not allowed to holiday right now—we have a major client presentation coming up. The one we need new ideas for."

"Did sitting in your boss's office work?"

"Nothing. Not a single thought. No wonder the Pope of Mope is such a blank page. Anyhow, Marcus and I forgot all about you until we heard a noise in the kitchen."

"That's okay," I said guiltily. "You found me."

He smiled again. "Which type of cookie did you choose? I'm guessing you chose a witch for the chocolate hair, right?"

"A ghost, actually. I'm all about vanilla."

"Interesting. Very, very interesting."

"They're really good, by the way. I was tempted so I'm glad it's okay I took one."

"Paulette will be pleased—she baked them herself. I know it's only October first, but she is such a fan of Halloween that she's decided it's a monthlong holiday. You'll meet her in a minute."

The mystery man motioned for me to follow him. He led me to a room I'd scouted out already, the one with the novelty hat rack. There were two other people in there now: a very tall man standing on his chair in a pirate hat and a woman at work on an art project.

"Is this the spy, Joel?" This loud question came from the pirate brandishing a plastic sword in my direction. "Spy!" he cried again after he fixed the plastic black eyepatch falling down over his left eye.

The fortyish woman was seated at a desk with a floating orange jack-o'-lantern balloon tied to an arm of her chair. She had a mass of red frizzy hair flying up over her ears like she was in the middle of bouncing on a trampoline. She was clearly ignoring the pirate. Her huge eyeglasses covered up her tiny nose as she scribbled furiously on shiny black paper.

No doubt about it: this place was wack. "I think I'm here at a bad time," I said to the man they called Joel. "I could go and come tomorrow. Come back when things are normalized?"

The woman looked up. "Normalized?" She smiled to herself and went back to work. Before I could fully process her comic face—was that her real hair or a clown's fright wig?—the tall pirate stomped his white sneaker and pointed at me with his sword. "Who are you? State your case!"

"I'm Jordie Popkin," I said tentatively.

"Louder!" All three of them screamed this together.

"I am Jordie Popkin! High school junior!" I couldn't believe that I'd just complied like that.

I mentally dubbed the would-be pirate Bluebeard. There was a skylight above us, so the rain clouds outside darkened the room. But even with dim light, one look at his long face and big chin told me he had to be my principal's brother. Becky Lee, the internship coordinator at my high school, had only yesterday informed me that a sibling connection with my principal was the reason this unusual internship was being offered to students at my math and science high school this year. I couldn't wait to tell my closest friends,

Jeremy and Clara: *Dr. D's brother was running around the room like a pirate, no BS!*

"Speak!" demanded Bluebeard. "Answer! What do you want to be when you grow up?" This guy was really pushing that corny pirate voice.

"I don't know yet, Captain," I replied.

"You don't want to be a scientist, then, lass?"

"No," I said. It felt so freeing to finally say that. The kooky mood in the room made me feel free to talk without holding back.

"Well then. I'm Marcus Herman," said the pirate in a much more normal voice. He opened a Krispy Kreme variety box and held out a half-dozen doughnuts. "You, new girl. First dibs."

"She'll have the vanilla one," Joel said just as I was about to reach for it.

"I'm guessing that you're my principal's brother," I said to Marcus a bit daringly after a bite. (My dad had always said that fearlessness is a great sell-yourself technique.)

"Guilty as charged. But don't hold that against me," Marcus said. "Delores was always the serious one in the family. To this day she sees absolutely nothing funny about the word *Uranus*."

I smiled. That little detail explained *so* much about my principal.

"Would you like something to drink?" Marcus said happily.

"We have everything in the kitchen," the frizzy-haired woman said with her eyes still focused on her artwork.

"Tang. Ovaltine. Quik. Kool-Aid," Marcus said.

"Thanks, I'll have a Coke," I said to Marcus. I was sure

that I could actually converse with him now that he'd dropped his dopey pirate accent.

Marcus looked at me like wanting a can of Coke was some kind of strange request.

"You want a soda? Joel, do we have any Cokes?"

"No, just banana and pineapple soda. But no more peach."

I ended up going with a neon yellow glass of repulsively sweet pineapple soda. Before I could take a second sip, the woman with the frizz do reached into a drawer of her cluttered desk and topped my drink with a pink paper parasol.

"I'm Paulette," she said, finally introducing herself. She smiled big as she stood up for a cat stretch in a stained shirt and ripped jeans. Now I could clearly see what she was working on. She was not scribbling, she was scratching. As she rose she rested her sharp X-Acto knife diagonally across a waxy black scratchboard card. She'd let some interesting colors emerge, and her design was some kind of rainbow-colored bird that, against the black background, appeared to be floating in space.

I smiled back at Paulette. "Good to meet you."

"So, you go to Manhattan Science. . . ."

Was that a question? "I do."

"Great. That's absolutely perfect because I have a science question for you. Do hummingbirds open their beaks?"

Joel threw his arms over his head. "Paulette!"

"*What?*" she drawled out in two syllables.

"Again with the hummingbirds? Just because they're tiny doesn't mean they don't have mouths. How else are they going to feed themselves and their babies?"

"I know the answer, though," I said. "My mom has a hummingbird calendar, and I've never noticed any beaks. I kind of thought they had a built-in straw to sip up the nectar."

"That's what I thought." Paulette beamed at me with a big gummy smile.

"Wrong and wrong." Joel shook his head furiously, but he was laughing at the same time.

"I'm not the one making mistakes today, Joel."

Joel looked right at me instead of Marcus. "My mistake? I sent our client a lovely bunch of flowers from an Internet florist."

"What's wrong with that?" I said.

Marcus took his seat. "Nothing wrong, unless you idiotically sent a funeral wreath because you were too busy talking when you were clicking!"

I laughed. They all smiled appreciatively in my direction and then looked at each other knowingly.

"The gig is yours if you want it," Marcus said. "We're all good judges of character here. Creatives are sensitive souls."

Paulette cringed at the last part of his comment, and added, slightly more formally, "You're exactly the person we want."

"I'm glad to hear that. What exactly do you *do* here? What would I be accepting? All I was told was that this is an ad agency of sorts."

"We dream up toys," Paulette said. "Not toys aimed at the upscale toy store buyers. That kind of toy is night and day from—"

"Just get it out," Joel said to Paulette with a curious look.

She hesitated for a second, but then loudly and proudly added, "We specialize in premiums."

"Oh, um . . ." I wasn't quite sure what she meant. Premium what?

My question was left hanging. Marcus leaned over to where Paulette was scraping her birdlike design and grabbed a square of origami-sized, mossy green tissue paper. He laid it on a comb he retrieved from his pocket and blew his impromptu, homemade kazoo.

"Answer her, Paulette," Marcus demanded.

Marcus stared at her. Finally he spoke instead. "We make the toys in Happy Boxes. Our boutique agency is number one in the fast-food toy premium business. We have only one serious competitor, out in Los Angeles."

15

"Oh," I said again, again drawing the word out of my mouth really slowly.

"Is there a problem?" Marcus asked.

Paulette watched me closely. "Do you have a moral issue with that?"

Did I? Her question prompted me to think a bit, and I discovered that I was relatively okay with it.

Yes, okay, a few toddlers might get a few too many greasy french fries in their system, but was I about to ponder the evils of corporate America when I had just been granted a get out of jail free card? Here I had thought that this was going to be some kind of dull pharmaceutical agency approved by Dr. D, and I was doomed to be Xeroxing copy about sinus and allergy pills. Marcus, Paulette, and Joel seemed warm, funny, and nice. This "real world" work experience veered so far from my school's stringent math and science mandate that my guess was that my internship coordinator didn't even know what Out of the Box marketed.

"Why should she have a moral issue with us?" Marcus snapped.

"It sounds out of the ordinary," I said with a real smile, and the three of them looked at me approvingly.

2. Situation Analysis

Know what you are working with. If you're
serious about selling your brand, take
stock. Why are you different? The best way
to find out is to go crazy with the details, and
you will discover that your written
thoughts answer these questions:
What are you working with here?
Are you smart? Are you a stylish dresser?
A fun person to be around?
What is your family like, and how has
that influenced your personality?
How did you get to be what you are today?
Where are you on the school social scale?
The golden rule at this stage
is to be BRUTALLY honest. (For real.)

Over the past few years my principal, the self-righteous Dr. Delores Herman—aka Dr. D—had made it clear that she thought none of her students should be allowed any unusual (i.e., cool) internships, like working for the inkers at Marvel comics or assisting the stylists at *Glamour* magazine—internships we'd jealously heard were offered at another of Manhattan's public magnet high schools. As far as my circle of friends was concerned, the three most desirable internships Dr. D had allowed for the students of Manhattan Science were: assistant to the NBC News medical reporter; production intern with the science show at WNYC, our local NPR radio station; and the spot at the *New York Times* with the science editor. But most of the "taste of the real world" junior year "jobs" involved things like filing with medical libraries and helping out in the administrative offices of hospitals. The kids who were really gunning to be scientists could duke it out for the assistant positions with big-name researchers, but that kind of work was not for my small artsy group of friends.

We really stood out, and were sometimes derided for it. All of the kids in our magnet school had a large vocabulary, so nobody ever got picked on just for being a brain. But even a school geared to spitting out future innovators in quantum mechanics and string theory has a social pecking order. Here, cheerleading and football were nonexistent, but guys like Vaughan Nussman and girls like Tara Jones were our version of the A-listers. They were often just as exceptional at math and science as the nerds, but they were also extremely attractive and social butterflies.

My friends were considered likeable B-listers. It was an okay existence. There are always going to be kids who have it worse in high school than anyone else, the really really unfortunate-looking girl your heart goes out to because none of the boys will talk to her, or the stringy-haired guy who never bathes who *no one* will talk to. I was in an average slot, not miserable but longing for an A-list guy. I was not really offensive to anyone, you know what I mean?

Every year across the five boroughs of New York City—Manhattan, Brooklyn, Queens, Staten Island, and the Bronx—there are thirteen-year-olds out celebrating when they find out they've gained admission to my renowned school. In an insanely expensive and competitive city, here's a school that every year sends over one hundred out of seven hundred seniors to an Ivy League college and costs parents absolutely nothing.

But I did not celebrate when I heard I got in. Hard to believe.

Back in eighth grade, I'd worked up the courage to admit to my parents that I didn't particularly want to apply to a renowned math and science school. I'd even asked if they possibly had enough money to keep me in Clarkson, my cozy little private school, which ran all the way up to twelfth grade.

"Your tuition is killing our finances," Mom had said after a long sigh.

"How about if I apply to Art and Design?"

"I'm not sending you to school to cut and paste. And why would you be any happier there? You've never expressed any real interest in art."

She had a point. If there had been a magnet school for writing and journalism, maybe she would have let me apply. But there wasn't an exclusive (and free) school like that in New York City. I mulled for hours over the status of the family bank account and what Mom had meant about "killing our finances." Although my mother likes to say, "Jordie never misses anything!" I didn't know one thing about how bad our family money situation was back then. We had family vacations. Bills got paid. Food was on the table.

"Are we actually broke?" I'd whispered to Dad as Mom took one of her usual forty-five-minute showers.

"It's been a hard year for sales," Dad had said with an embarrassed nod. "The economy's gone *kaplunk*."

"I heard that some public schools have over fifty kids in a room. What kind of attention can a teacher give a kid with numbers like that?" I asked Mom another time.

"It doesn't matter, if every one of those kids can challenge you at lunch," Mom had said. "Your sister went to Manhattan Science without complaint."

"Sari was dying to go. She wants to be a scientist."

"And look how she excelled. The school makes special effort to lead girls into jobs that women have always been cut off from."

Even today my mother snaps out of any conversation that mentions the word *fun*.

Not me. I've loved fun for as long as I can remember. I desperately wanted to have unicorns for my eighth birthday party theme and was obsessed with a goofy and huge unicorn piñata in our local party store. Mom's big happy idea for the birthday party, however, was that I should insist my little girlfriends dress as lab scientists and she would decorate my birthday cake with test tubes and plastic white mice. No kidding—and she did it.

Most kitchens have sweet breakfast place mats with garden vegetables or a motif of oil and vinegar cruets, right?

My mother hand-made our place mats, laminating the periodic table of elements. The maddening thing is, it worked. It's ingrained. I can still tell you, after hundreds of bowls of Cheerios and Raisin Bran, that number 26, Fe, is iron; 33, As, is Arsenic; and 95, Am, is americium.

Believe me, that was the tip of the iceberg. Mom took many extra steps to introduce science to her girls because it was her agenda. According to my father, Mom's mother (Grandma Barbara) thwarted Mom's dreams of becoming a famous scientist like Nobel Prize winner Marie Curie. The children of the Jersey City branch of the Fischers were poor and smart. Mom and her little sister (Aunt Deborah) had to work so their brother (Uncle Peter) could afford college tuition for physics. He did well in school and went to work for NASA at Cape Canaveral. Uncle Peter was literally a rocket scientist while my jealous mother had to redirect her science skills into a sometimes disturbingly logic-based theory of parenting.

Now, years later, Mom had a good job writing educational science materials for elementary schools. But I knew that despite her many accomplishments, her brother's many laurels silently devastated her. NASA gave Uncle Peter a special award once for career achievement, and astronauts came for cocktails. Uncle Peter kept saying to everyone that it was my mom who really had "the knack" for science in his family, and that how she never ended up in the field still amazed him. Whenever anyone privately asked her what her genius brother was like growing up, Mom bizarrely offered him or her a peppermint Chiclet.

Thus, with double guilt over money and Mom's dreams for me, I gave it my all.

My surprisingly okay math score (how the bleep did that happen!) coupled with an exceedingly high English score got me in. I passed by just three points. But in is in.

* * *

Switching schools from middle school to high school must be petrifying for anyone. But going from my coddled little world to a huge public magnet school was a real trauma.

Now there were seven hundred people in my grade, as opposed to fifty-one. And as my family's rent-controlled apartment building has no doorman, at Clarkson I had been on the lower end of the economic scale. I soon found out at Manhattan Science that a poorer kid at a fancy school still meant my family had money. That was the biggest eye-opener of my transfer. For the first time in my life some of my classmates were from housing projects. If they passed the entrance exam, they could come. Money supposedly didn't matter at Manhattan Science; but keeping up your test scores certainly did.

I immediately loved the surprising fact that being fabulously dressed and stupid was not tolerated at my new school. At Clarkson, one of my classmates was a beautiful daughter of movie stars who was always in danger of failing everything. She never bothered to read a word of *The Catcher in the Rye*. She got six Fs in seventh grade, but her parents donated a new wooden floor for the gym. In the fall there she was back at school again, her teachers baffled and slightly annoyed at the sight of her.

But without a good friend, the first weeks of freshman year at Manhattan Science were frightening. Wending my way from overwhelming class to overwhelming class, I was more than mildly freaked, beyond convinced that I would never pass the tough goals each teacher had passed out on day one. I desperately needed one good friend to get over the shy hump. All was well after I met Clara Langostini.

It was a case of instant best friendship. Clara had her locker near mine and pointed out she had the same Danish school bag that I had. It was a relief to have anyone besides a teacher communicating with me, and I instantly became Super Talky Girl. I confessed that I had searched online, tormenting myself over what bookbag would be coolest for a new school. Her warm smile was reassuring after she whispered, "So did I!" We had lunch that day in the back of the cafeteria. Clara admitted that she'd also taken the Manhattan Science test to please her struggling middle-class parents, and that she also wanted to be a journalist one day.

Later on in the year, people couldn't believe we hadn't met until ninth grade. "You seem like sisters," they'd say all the time.

Over the years, Clara and I experienced many important moments together.

Of course, part of being a best friend was sharing everything you heard being said about each other, bad or good. That was another one of our important pacts we always honored, most recently a week before junior internships started. In between classes when I was about to enter French class on the second floor, Clara called me from the fifth floor on my cell. She was whispering something, and the phone connection was staticky. "I can't hear a freaking word, Clara. Tell me in five."

When she was standing before me, I said, "So, what's the big news?"

Turns out she had waited for the crush of stair traffic to subside so she could retie her sneaker, and she'd overheard other stragglers talking in the echoey stairwell a floor above

her. Her ears perked because she heard my name. The only two notably cute guys from the math team, Mark Bruin and Doug Erps, were ranking the returning class, and using very precise math team calculations gave me an 8.57 out of a possible 10 on desirability, doing a mean of looks, intelligence, and sense of humor. She admitted they gave Virginia Kline a 9.34, and Tara Jones an uncontested 10—but we both thought that 8.57 was pretty good, and frankly about the same number we then gave both of the rankers. (Except we rounded our numbers.)

To keep the high of being respectably desirable, I didn't ask Clara if they'd given her a score. I had good reason to be nervous, as Clara is definitely prettier than I am. That's just a cold fact. Her dark blond hair was trimmed with short bangs that accentuated her perfectly proportioned heart-shaped face.

My second best friend at Manhattan Science was the wisecracking Jeremy Hart, a tall, deep-voiced guy who Clara introduced me to the first week of school—she had gone to a public middle school with him in Greenwich Village. I asked Jeremy how he'd changed since seventh and eighth grades, and Clara demanded that her old pal confess he'd talked ridiculously in a high, squeaky voice even though his voice changed earlier than everyone else's.

"I sounded like one of those Chipmunks cartoons," he said in a baritone. And then he laughed louder than both of us did.

By sophomore year the Hernandez twins transferred in after passing the test on their second try. I shared my history class with both of them and introduced them to Clara and

Jeremy. The siblings were born in the Dominican Republic, and their English scores were the reason that they had barely missed two spots in the freshman class. Willie and Blanca, who lived with their mom in a housing project in Spanish Harlem, got a perfect score on every math exam. Despite their easy math grades, they both desperately wanted to be jazz musicians. Willie was the one who told me math and music are complementary skills. He confessed once that he was not allowed to apply to the High School for Performing Arts. His mother wanted her twins to be professionals—a lawyer, a doctor, almost anything but a musician.

In a public math and science school, a kind of radar thing exists if you're there for the free tuition or for your parents' pride and not for yourself.

The waywards always find each other.

3. Target Market

You must determine your target market.
Who exactly is your market?
A forward-thinking creative might hire an
anthropologist or a sociologist.
But sometimes a budget is small and
you need to be that anthropologist.
Once you've selected the guy you want,
it's time to focus on him.
Study his wardrobe. Who are his friends?
What makes him tick?
Once you've isolated your audience,
make sure you're near him.
Can you go to the same event?
Can you orchestrate time away
from your competition?
Get close to your target.

One of the first phrases you hear used in the marketing world is *target market*. I can safely say that at the beginning of junior year there was no other target market for me besides Vaughan Nussman. I lusted for him, to put it mildly, but alas, so did Clara, so did every other girl in our grade. But I'd basically accepted he was still barely aware of me— even though the precalculus class he was in with me in the afternoon was not the first class we'd had together.

Vaughan Nussman.

1. It's not enough to say he was merely a good-looking blue-eyed blond.

2. He had deep-set blue eyes that were *hypnotic*.

3. His lips were really big and red. Think young Elvis lips.

4. His nice-sized nose had just a bit of a bump that gave

him real character, not one of those cutesy button noses like you see on gooey guys in boy bands.

5. His hair was long, not greasy long, but fashionably funky without any evidence of hair product. He had dazzling white teeth, and a dimple on one of his cheeks.

6. Every time he opened his mouth, he seemed very confident. His voice had none of the unevenness about it that his adolescent classmates suffered from.

7. As far as I could tell, he was zit free. Nobody I knew, even the other A-listers, were zit free.

8. He was extremely fit, with muscles. In fact, I never saw him with a gangly physique, even in ninth grade. One late spring afternoon in second-semester freshman year, I saw Vaughan do a one-arm pushup in the nearby park when he thought no one was looking. He was very pleased with his own strength, and his confidence in himself was really sexy. All the other sixteen-year-olds I knew were constantly apologizing for what they said to me. Vaughan must have gone through puberty in elementary school.

What kind of teen boy never gets a zit or a cracked voice?

9. A Greek god, maybe.

There was also another guy in precalculus who I semi-had on my radar, Zane Minton. Zane was tall, but unlike Vaughan he was very quiet, so quiet that I knew very little about him—except that he was always bright in class and after a rather rocky hormonal start our freshman year he had turned out surprisingly good-looking. No one I knew had the scoop on Zane. He was one of those blushers who made me feel a bit uncomfortable for not being afflicted with that problem. His cheeks turned purple every time he talked to anyone of the female sex. Personally, I was still a little shocked every time I heard Zane speak. Back when we were all fourteen, Zane had straight blond hair, was four or so inches shorter, and occasionally squeaked when he talked. But his hair had darkened to a sandy brown and curled as puberty kicked in. I knew it wasn't a perm or anything, because that's what my father says happened to him when he was teenager. Now Zane was all the more awkward, as his new tall frame had not filled in yet with muscle. Clara acknowledged that he was cute, but she dismissed him as just far too awkward. Still, I kind of wanted to hold his hand whenever he addressed me, which was rarely.

4. Create the Right Team

A winning team helps.
Not everybody can afford to hire
the best in the business, but there is
something you can do. You can wear
different hats, pretending you have
different team members in the room.
Yes, it's worth a try.
Just like back in the doll days.
(But this time it won't be cute if
your mother hears you,
so make sure your door is closed.)

"I like the place," I said once again to my mother the night of my internship offer from Out of the Box. "What's so bad about *enjoying* something to do with school for a change?"

"Ask your coordinator for something other than hamburger premiums."

"All of the other good internships are already filled, and that's not my fault."

"Are you saying it's my fault?"

Well, yes, I thought. Maybe I would still have had a chance of landing my first choice work experience internship—the science desk of the *New York Times*—if I hadn't been sick with a fever. I tried to go to school for my counseling session, got showered and dressed in time, but Mom had kept repeating "one hundred and two degrees" like a mantra in a yoga studio. She went to work but made my father stand guard as her stand-in naysayer. He'd literally sat in front of our door as he fired up his laptop.

What I said instead was "You really want me to be stuck in an arctic-cold room with a bunch of nude dead bodies?"

"Please, cut the drama. No high school on Earth would send a kid to work in a morgue."

"I'm not being dramatic!" I practically wailed.

"There actually is a morgue internship, Mom," Sari interjected in her calm, measured voice. "Forensic science gets the nod from Dr. D."

I pointed to Sari like a worked-up contestant on reality TV. "See, stop ragging on me, Mom! Sari knows I'm not lying!"

"You know as well as I do that unless you had a burning desire to work in a morgue, they would never make you go. All I want you to do is call and see if there's something more serious available. Something more . . . career furthering. Something that will actually benefit humanity."

How else could I convince my always-knows-best Mom what a dire situation she'd placed me in by making me stay home in bed while Jeremy and Clara no doubt charmed the pants off the editors at the *Times*? Was there even a chance now for the *Times* interview at such a late date?

Jeremy had a 96 average and was Mr. Likeable, while Clara was a very talented writer just like her mother, who wrote for nonprofit consumer magazines. With sharp competition like my very own friends for the only internships I wanted, I was doomed. I'd personally have hired them both in a flash.

So instead of being stuck in a boring office—surely my

destiny if I was up against them—I decided that I *needed* to get that funky premiums internship. I had the court advantage, as Jeremy would say.

Sari was home because she was on one of those week-long breaks college students get all the time for no particular reason. Well, my only hope was to get Mom's pet to knock some sense into her.

Once upon a time Sari and I were very close. When I was eleven, we smooched the fridge, and she told me I'd be a good kisser since the kissy lipstick marks on the door were impressively even. I sometimes braided her hair for her, and vice versa. Even if we broke out in catfights all the time, wasn't that still a sign of a working sisterhood?

But then, once Sari hit high school, she achieved in a massive way, and this weird kindness tainted by a superior air set in.

Mom was forever accusing me of being her drama queen teen. Even when I was little she called me her "expressive" child.

I thought some more about a lost opportunity to have fun and learn something. I burst out with "Can't you just listen to what I want once, Mom? Once! Not insist on what *you* want for me?"

"When have I ever done that?" she demanded quietly.

"The unicorns, Mom."

"What unicorns?"

"The lab scientist party," Sari said neutrally. "Jordie wanted unicorns."

Mom shook her head at me. "You're crazy. That party was fabulous."

I moaned. "No, it was not. Not to eight-year-old girls. That party was humiliating."

Her mouth crimped.

Where do you go with an argument after you've already brought up the morgue and yearned-for unicorns and received zero sympathy? I lay on the corner of my bed in the fetal position.

Mom threw her thin arms up in the air. "Uncoil, Jordie. You'll hurt your back."

"There's always a sciencey Goth kid who's dying to take that morgue slot," Sari offered. I could tell Sari genuinely thought she was helping, even as she poured cold water on my protest. "You'll get a good one if you hang in there. They'll love you on the internship interviews. Little Miss Lively."

Yeah, thanks a lot, team player. "I missed out on the interviews!" I said quickly to curb this horribly chipper line of thought. "This is one of the only okay ones left—maybe the only one!"

But Sari was not done with her interference. "You could always do the internship I had. The colleges I applied to loved it. I'll call Harry to see if he has selected someone yet. Even if he has, maybe he'll want another Popkin."

"That's a good idea, Sari," Mom said. "See? Problem solved."

I grimaced. My sister's high school work experience internship was with Dr. Harry Finneran, a Nobel Prize–winning biologist at Columbia University. I've never exactly followed what she did for him, but it had something to do with analyzing the behavior of adolescent dung beetles.

Sometimes I can't believe I incubated in the same womb as her.

"That was great for you, but I'm not the science whiz. It'd never work out."

Sari shrugged her shoulders again. "I'm sure with my pull you could get it."

With Nobel Prize Harry's raving recommendation he wrote for Sari's college applications, six of the Ivies were desperate to get my sister to enroll. Who the hell gets to knock back Harvard? Sari did. She chose Princeton because the administration was willing to give her a free ride all the way through to graduation. Free as in free—all expenses paid. I found out about this incredible development halfway through my freshman year at our high school. It was a Saturday afternoon. Sari had already been accepted to Cornell and Dartmouth, so my jealousy was raging high that week and I had escaped to Clara's apartment to confess. We had a blast together fabric-painting our jeans.

When I returned home and opened the front door, my father was crying over Sari's even more magnificent news like he'd just won the Powerball lottery.

An hour after the toy premiums internship fight with my mother, Dad broke up my self-pity party when he poked his head into my room with a loopy smile from taking too much cold medicine. "Jordie, can you wiggle the loose cable wire? I need your magic touch."

Without any real aid from Sari, I knew that keeping far away from Mom was the best thing for my boiling-over resentment. So I figured I'd help Dad—there is something about our apartment cable reception doesn't like. This temperamental TV's days were numbered. We would soon have TiVo and all the magic that came with a larger coaxial cable; Dad had just placed an order for it that morning, a gift to himself for his upcoming fiftieth birthday.

As I fiddled with the cable wire until the reception came in clearly, I asked myself how my mother was still allowed to order me around like a three-year-old. I personally thought I could learn a lot at Out of the Box.

It was such a lost cause that it wasn't even worth fighting. Mom is not someone you want to go more than one round with. And frankly, I was scared that what I'd like to say to her next would get me in the doghouse big-time. Sari, our budding biologist, had recently likened me to toxic sea snakes in Indonesia, underwater serpents that supposedly descended from one family of Australian land snakes. One of her friends in college was studying them. She said that when the snakes get prodded with sticks by scuba divers, they'd take it for a time but then suddenly turn around and charge.

I did feel like charging. I was a creative person about to be forced into an unthinkably dull semester at some stupid medical company.

Didn't my mother even listen to me last week when I told her how I was part of a group of students who made an appointment with our principal to widen the scope of offerings? Apparently not.

She had been ironing her work clothes when I further explained that my friends had designated Jeremy to be our main negotiator. All Mom had actually said that day was that she thought me "very modern" for staying friends with my ex-boyfriend.

Boyfriend? I haven't mentioned that little tidbit about Jeremy yet. Well, truthfully, it was—as my father's mother, Grandma Pearl, would say—"a tame affair." It's a little easier to hang with your ex when you only went out for three days, three long all-about-the-Knicks days. That is to say, Jeremy is an *extreme* sports nut, and asking him even one basketball question (just to be polite, mind you) is like entering a hypertext world gone very wrong. Back in freshman geology, Jeremy was amazingly helpful during exam time. He offered to help me with whatever I wasn't getting. His study methodology was priceless; he'd explain everything on Earth, including the birth of Earth itself, in terms of either football or basketball. We were both enrolled in a mandatory geology class taught by Mr. Munson, a man who frequently shed small drops of disgusting dribble onto our homework assignments before he handed them back. I never knew what to do with my damp returned homework, so as soon as I was out the door I'd drop it by my fingertips into the garbage bin in the lobby of our school. This biweekly purging turned out to be an idiotic move; when it came time to study for our midterm, Munson announced that it would be based entirely on the old homeworks. Jeremy assured me that I would still be okay if I used his signature sports-reference memory techniques. "Picture all the gas and dust floating around as the players at a Cowboys-Redskins game. One bad play and there's a huge pileup at the scrimmage line—and that's when you get a planet."

"You're *incredible*," I'd said sincerely.

Out of the blue he kissed me after that compliment!

But it all too quickly felt too friendshipy. Maybe his penchant for onion rolls and Tabasco-flavored Slim Jim and Mango Xtremo Gatorade had something to do with our fast breakup—who was I to suggest a breath mint at the three-day relationship mark?—but mostly I couldn't handle going out with a sports fanatic, and I simply told him so. My ever getting intensely interested in televised team sports was and is about as likely as a construction worker wanting to know all about pirouettes.

Jeremy was tall when I met him, with the same deep voice, but his body wasn't fully cooked yet. One summer away, another blast of hormonal action, and even Blanca was calling him a stud. But Clara and I still privately felt, as far as his boyfriend suitability went, his obsession with televised sports canceled out his looks.

Almost three years since our blinked-and-you'd-missed-it freshman-year romance, Jeremy and I were still safely in *friendship territory*—even if once in a while I was amazed to see how built he'd become under my nose. I could see other girls whispering about him when he walked toward me on the street.

He could have had any of the many acceptable B-list girls (besides me and Clara). But Jeremy had another flaw besides his sports mania: overconfidence.

* * *

Our meeting with Dr. D to widen internship opportunities was a fiasco. It was my fault in a way, as I'd backed up Jeremy when he said he was the best suited to talk for all of us. "Absolutely, Jeremy should go first. He's the only one who could do this right—he's on varsity debate."

I think Jeremy wanted to speak passionately mainly because he was dying to intern with the announcers for the New York Knicks. He was disgusted by the "horrifically dull" internship choices, and with six of us artsy types in tow, he demanded action.

"Dr. Herman, there are at least one hundred juniors who signed up for junior internship this semester. However, there are only seven or so positions available that I, or anyone in this room for that matter, would be happy to score. We have other interests that we'd like to explore as career possibilities, and we hope that the school would help us in that direction."

Dr. D clucked her tongue in horror and shook her head. "Did you say '*score*'? This is a hallowed school for kids who excel in math and science." She stuck her chin out as she spoke down to us. "If you are here for any other reason than for our official mandate, that's not my responsibility. English does not appear to be one of your strengths, regardless."

For the next twenty minutes Dr. D breathed dragon fire and stared us down with her scary green eyes. She refused to acknowledge that a good chunk of her students, at least 10 percent of us, like me, had gotten into her "hallowed school" by acing the vocabulary and reading comprehension—not math—and accepted a spot to save our parents money on private school tuition. (English counts for half the test at Manhattan Science, just like on the SATs.)

After the catastrophic meeting, we huddled outside her closed door. Jeremy was the most depressed, and ashamed to look any of us in the face. "I can't believe I used that word."

I put my finger to my lips. Dr. D could have been listening.

School was over for the day, so we regrouped on the stoop of a brownstone across the street from our school, the only one on the block where the residents would let students sit. "What Dr. D really meant," would-be novelist Clara said, "is that anyone who doesn't dream of being a Nobel Prize–winning scientist can rot in their creative juices."

Tara Jones, the Manhattan Science perfect 10, overheard us talking. She was leaning against the railing of the stoop, taking advantage of the same hangout spot. She was in another conversation with some other stunning girl I didn't know, probably a senior, but she turned around and scolded us in her Alabaman accent. "Listen to y'all talk!" Her ponytail swished as she ripped into us. "Y'all are spoiled rotten," she said again, her venom glossed over by Southern charm.

I wish I could say that she cared more about her split ends than her schoolwork, but the truth is, she famously had a nearly perfect academic average as well as a stunning face and body.

Even though the sky was gray and the strong, cold fall wind was blowing yellow and orangey leaves sideways toward our stoop, Tara was dressed in a miniskirt that rose high above her pale knees. She paused midlecture to wet her chapped lips with her tongue.

"How can you say that, Tara?" Jeremy took the opportunity to chime in, and then nervously chewed his pinkie cuticle. There was an even bigger rumor about Tara than the one about her grade point average. Supposedly, not long after she moved to New York to be a model, she already earned more money than her mother and father combined. I heard that juicy tidbit from Jeremy himself, who reported on her every move. Boy, did Jeremy have it bad. Worse than I had it for Vaughan, which was pretty bad, let me tell you. The crazy thing was that Jeremy did not have a girlfriend because of Tara. Many girls in our class would have been delighted to be asked out by him; I'd fielded enough gushy questions to be sure of that. But Jeremy was ridiculously, futilely, holding out for Tara and staying "available."

Even though I was technically his ex-girlfriend, he'd had no hesitation admitting the week before that he had lusted for her since the day she transferred into the school in tenth grade, a year after we broke up. He claimed that in his oceanography class she spat out micrometric knowledge like C-3PO. "And this is from a girl so gorgeous that she could model a potato sack and get me hot."

Tara rolled her eyes at Jeremy, an action that must have wounded him severely. "How can I say that? Do you think anyone in Alabama even knows what an internship is? Y'all are worried about filing at a major metropolitan hospital, and where I come from you're lucky if your boobs are big enough to get you an after-high-school job at Hooters. Otherwise it's McDonald's or the garage."

Jeremy nodded, a pathetic guy in love. He couldn't believe

Tara was not already hooked up with Vaughan or one of the other hotly desired boys in our school—like Perry Nelson, the way-hip senior class editor of our school paper.

As several drops of rain fell on my head, I smiled with all my will and told her she had a point, so that Jeremy wouldn't rail against me later. But I was still fighting mad about the diminished opportunities, because this is New York and not rural Alabama, and I sure as hell had not landed a Ford Models contract that makes me that much more interesting to the male student body, and I didn't have the knack for oceanography that Harvard seems to want in students at the age of sixteen.

"It's classes like oceanography that really impress the college recruiters," I once overheard Dr. D say.

Tara may have come from "the real world," as she re-peatedly said, but Manhattan Science was *my* real world, and between parental and school expectations, this world was a pressure cooker. Tara looked to better herself, and here I was teamed with my friends, fighting for what we wanted too. I'm sorry, but we were born into this New York madness. We'd known nothing different. Who was she to judge us?

What would she say if she'd known how much I was willing to fight for a good internship? Something derogatory, no doubt.

The next day, per my promise to my mother, I headed to the internship counselor to see what I could find besides the agency spot. I had to wait, as there was a student being coun-seled in her office and the door was shut.

I read the flyer posted on the memo board outside Becky's door, a notice about the upcoming junior class Halloween dance. Most school dances were unanimously regarded as too cheesy for a downtown Manhattan high school—of course we had a senior prom, but there was no junior prom, and no one was asking for it—but the junior Halloween dance was a bona fide big deal, a chance through costume selection to show off how killer ironic you were.

Usually it fell on a weekday, but this year it fell on a Saturday, so word was that it was going to be *dee*-luxe.

Becky's door opened.

The kid being counseled turned out to be Jeremy.

"What did you get?" I whispered before entering Becky's office.

He pointed to the door with his thumb. "Well, I'm not getting the best vibe from her about the *Times*. I'm sure I'll get stuck with some administrative hell."

"I wish I even got an opportunity to interview for it."

"Oh, that's right, you were sick. Bad luck." He winced. "Do you think Clara could have gotten the internship?"

"She's not saying."

He rolled his eyes—she hadn't said anything about her internship interviews to either of us. It was simply not like her to play her cards so close to her chest. I was too anxious to ask, for what I might hear: "Oh, the *Times*, didn't I tell you—?"

Jeremy pointed to the dance flyer. "Do you think Tara would go if I asked her?"

"You're really going to ask me that?"

"Sorry. I'm just working up my courage."

"Good luck there. You'll need it." I admittedly said that rather obnoxiously. But even if he had a few gal fans among my junior class ranks, this was Tara the Cover of *Seventeen* Model we were talking about. The boy needed a reality check.

"Haven't you heard, Popkin? Beautiful girls never get asked out on dates."

"Was that payback?" I said in a jokingly accusatory way.

"What do you mean?"

"Was that an insult? Are you saying I'm not beautiful?"

I hissed at him like an angry snake, and he play-punched me. Then he very nicely kissed me on the cheek, and whispered, "Are you fishing for a compliment?"

"Yes."

"Then I'll give you one. You're very pretty, honey."

"Thank you." I smiled. "Even if that was a face-saving fudge."

Becky craned her head out and we knew she'd seen the kiss, but she didn't say anything except "Next."

"Okay," Becky said with such little enthusiasm that I wasn't really worried she had even registered a potential school gossip item. "So where are we with you?"

"I visited the toy premium company."

"Oh, right. I am happy to report they *loved* you."

"Well, I need something else. My mother won't let me take it."

She looked at me and sighed. "Come back after ninth period and we will discuss it."

I looked at my watch. Two p.m. Time for another eyeful of the sublimely gorgeous Vaughan.

* * *

"Hey, Zane," Vaughan said as he sat down and shoved the wayward bit of his wavy very-blond hair behind his ear, "how did your internship interview go?"

Were Vaughan and Zane friends? I remember thinking how odd that would be.

"Good, I think."

"I'm pretty certain I aced my interview at the NYU Medical Center emergency room."

"I'd think the emergency room would be nerve-racking," Zane said in a surprisingly relaxed voice.

Maybe not friends, I reevaluated. And perhaps Zane talked much more easily with guys.

Vaughan, as smart as he was handsome, was determined for Zane to see why an emergency room internship was the most happening spot of all. "Maybe so, but Harvard's going to eat this up. If you want to be a doctor, what better place to learn? There wasn't a down moment when I was there. Hey, where is yours again?"

"I'm going for the Finneran research spot at Columbia. A bit more low-key."

"Cool," Vaughan said. Since I knew all about Finneran, I tried to focus on what Zane was saying for a bit, but it was hard not to think about Vaughan's bright blue sweater, which brought out his awesome eyes.

"My sister had that internship three years ago," I piped up.

"Really?" Zane's neck was already turning color.

"She loved it."

"Are you applying there too?" he said nervously.

51

"I was sick, so I haven't had all of my interviews yet. I have my counseling meeting with Becky this afternoon. But honestly, I wasn't thinking of Finneran as an option."

Jeremy had been eavesdropping on my eavesdrop.

"Well, stay clear of the *Times*, Popkin. I'm dreading you telling me you sweet-talked Becky into a last-minute interview. You're my biggest threat, you know."

"She is?" Vaughan said.

"Are you kidding? Jordie could be the best writer in our grade."

At those complimentary words, one of Vaughan's brown eyebrows shot up. "Really?" I wasn't thrilled with his dumbfounded look. I could tell he didn't take me too seriously, which was a bit ego-shattering, as this dismissal was coming from the very guy I desired most. And I wasn't used to anyone sizing me up as a ditz. Back in Clarkson, I was always top of the class with Mindy Neiman.

Unfortunately, Vaughan had never seen me shine in my English classes, where I routinely got a "FANTASTIC!" comment on my papers.

You should probably know about my old English class.

At the end of sophomore year, my English teacher asked if she could send in an essay of mine to the National Council of Teachers of English for something called the Achievement Award in Writing. I was totally thrilled because Mrs. Kleinman had a lot of kids who hung on her every word. Mrs. Kleinman's tiny build—she was barely five feet tall—and her light blue eyes gave her a bit of a fairylike presence. But it was her calm, friendly smile and way of speaking to students without condescending to us that made her everybody's favorite English teacher.

"What shall we enter, Jordie?"

I'd liked that she said 'we,' that she thought of us as a team. I had thought about it all night and suggested both my "faux fairy tale," in which Cinderella falls for the coachman instead of the prince, as well as my character study of my neighbor's white poodle, who terrorized my apartment building floor before she died in a dogfight in our lobby—she thought she was a pit bull. But Mrs. Kleinman thought they were both too cutesy for this kind of competition.

I had been a bit offended at the word "cutesy." "Even with Princess's tragic end?"

"Even with." In the end, the essay "we" sent in was the one we had to model on articles you would find in a specialty magazine. Of course Jeremy chose *Sports Illustrated*, but I had chosen to write like a reporter from *Spin* magazine. I explained the contemporary music scene, and how my fellow teens in the twenty-first century wrongly worship the late 1970s British punk rockers as pioneers, when in fact punk rock was invented in *America* by a privileged group of private school kids like Television's Richard Hell and Tom Verlaine—and in the *early* 1970s. My essay suggested that because in England the musicians who took to the music actually were disadvantaged kids, the realness of their venom is why the American punk bands are side notes.

Even though the essay was entirely in my own words, I had gotten the ideas from some books on punk rock phenomena that my dad had given me. He claimed he played in

53

a punk band while at college, as hard as that was to believe. (If you knew my dad, you would drop your jaw too.) I thought what I had written was ultimately a bit too dry to be good reading, but Mrs. Kleinman vehemently disagreed. She felt it sounded both mature and written from a teen perspective, and demonstrated an appreciation of music history. She was confident it was exactly the style the judges were looking for.

Vaughan had never been in *any* of my four high school English classes to date—classes where I was a teacher's pet and almost always got admiring comments on my work from my classmates. No, the only extended time he'd spent around me previous to our current precalculus class was freshman-year algebra—a class that I passed only at the mercy of my teacher, who knew I was trying hard.

"So you're one of those?" Vaughan said after Jeremy's praise of my writing ability was over. Wendy Thayer was right; Vaughan's light blue eyes did have the slightest tint of purple to them.

"One of what?" Like Wendy, I was shocked that he had addressed me directly.

"The literary bohemians."

"If she gets an internship at the *Times*," Zane managed, "I'd hardly call that being a bohemian."

"Like I said, I was sick, so I'm probably not even going to get a chance to interview for it."

Vaughan ran his hand through his waves and sniffed openly. "You know, I did commercials when I was kid." (As if I didn't know. Thanks to Wendy, who did an obsessive search on the Internet for any site with Nussman "Vaughan" in it, every girl in school knows Vaughan was the little boy in the Golden Grahams cereal commercial.) "My mother," he continued, "wanted me to stick with Professional Children's School. She thought all I'm good for is acting. I insisted I go here. There have been eighteen Nobel scientists who graduated from here."

"I've heard."

I'm not sure Vaughan picked up on the growing edge in my voice, because he lectured on: "Scientists can change the world and save lives. We are privileged to get the training we get here. I would never opt for the easy way out. I want my time on Earth to count."

"I don't see working for the *Times* or NPR as the easy way out," Zane said.

"That's not what I meant," Vaughan huffed.

"What did you mean?" Zane asked quietly.

"I mean about my mom's plan for me to be an actor."

"Some of us aren't here for the science," I said. "Some of us are here because of our parents. And we'd like the chance to follow our own passions. The media internships are the closest thing to literature and creative writing, what *I'm* interested in."

Vaughan gave me a long, condescending look before he spoke again. "You really think you could land those places, anyway?"

I took a deep breath. He really thought I was an airhead!

Well, he was sitting two rows in front of me, and I was very publicly foundering once again in a math class. But this time I had no kindly teacher willing to take mercy. My mother showed no mercy either when she "accidentally" fished an early-semester math test out of my bag. "What kind of a student gets a ninety-eight in English and a sixty-eight on her math exam?"

A student who never wanted to go to math and science school, Mom. But of course I didn't say that.

And what I really wanted to say to Vaughan—*You don't know me!*—I didn't say either.

If you really don't know someone well, deriding them is like making a decision from chopped-off data.

In those long seconds before the class officially started, I was torn between despising him and leaning over and forcing a kiss. Did you ever have that mixed feeling, being attracted to someone you hate? Thankfully, the new-period bell rang, and our grumpy teacher, Mr. Etchingham, asked for our homework. "Pass it up, pass it up. No scribbling in now! I'll mark anyone who scribbles now as a cheater."

Etchingham's close-cropped hair and deep voice always made him very intimidating. But on this day, as he inched along the front-row seats in a stained red Izod shirt, he precisely reminded me of a big scary crab on the beach moving sideways down the sand. As lousy as my assignment was—I'd left two questions blank—I gratefully let him clamp his claw down on my homework.

56

5. Improvisation— An Art Worth Learning

Occasionally, a good marketer
must make it up as she goes alon
Don't ever be idle—just do someth
Action is better than regret.
So buckle up.

5. Improvisation— An Art Worth Learning

Occasionally, a good marketer
must make it up as she goes along.
Don't ever be idle—just do something!
Action is better than regret.
So buckle up.

At the end of the day when I entered Becky's office again, she had a huge mug of coffee in her hand. She looked like she'd rather be anywhere than in her office swamped with overflowing paperwork. Even though it was not a hot day, her face was covered with sweat.

"Okay, now I have time to talk this through. So why not take the slot at Out of the Box? When I said they *loved* you, I meant it."

"I told you. My mom is"—I stopped to make quotation marks in the air—" 'bitterly opposed' to my working there."

Exasperated, she put her hands in the air. "Bitterly opposed? It sounds so much more fun than anything else I'm offering. And you're the first and only one I've sent over there. You're the one I think is perfect—"

"That's so nice, but Mom thinks I should aim higher, see if there are other choices."

"Well, I'm sorry to say you're one of the last to be placed. There isn't much else there for you. I just did my assignments, and there are only two open places—"

"What are they? I'd love to go to the *Times* if that one is still open." Who was I kidding? How could that be left?

"Are you kidding?" Becky said after a big sip of her coffee. "Taken. They grabbed one of the students they liked right away. They're too busy to interview anyone else."

"Who got it?" I said a bit shakily. "Jeremy Hart? Clara Langostini?" Even if Clara was my best friend, I knew she would be unbearable if she scored that internship. And I wasn't sure I could mask my jealousy.

"Wait for the posting."

"Is the NBC science reporter one available?"

"Assigned."

I could tell by her face that every "good" internship was gone.

"Medicine is an exciting field," she tried. "We still have an opening there, maybe even two. Our local hospital contacts are eager for our student interns. They like them better than some of the college kids they get."

"I really hate blood," I said truthfully. "I'd faint. Isn't there anything left?"

"Let's scratch that opening at the NYU Medical Center emergency room, then. They've already filled one slot, but there are two because one of the doctors there went to Manhattan Science."

My heart raced as Becky answered her phone.

"Yes, Zane is a very bright kid. I'm so glad you liked him, Dr. Finneran. . . ."

I was happy for Zane, but I was even more focused on that double emergency room slot. This was insider trading! Forget hamburger premiums! I could intern with Vaughan, one on one, with no other girls from class as distraction. I'd set his arrogant mind straight—I'd show him how smart I was as I helped the doctors in distress. In a split second my mind seesawed between the pros and cons. Could I really handle that environment? I learned how to rollerblade the previous summer. I quickly told myself, *Oh, c'mon, I'd eventually get the handle on high-end stress.* When I'm relaxed, I'm bubbly. He'd laugh a lot. I'd sashay around the hospital in my new sexy black skirt and spangly red shirt from H&M. Okay, maybe not a spangly shirt in the emergency room, but maybe my new low-cut jeans from Urban Outfitters. I'd win the hunk over, we'd hook up, and then I'd tease him that he ever thought I could be vacuous. Then I'd dump the self-righteous snob.

61

"Did Zane get it?" I asked when Becky hung up. She was positively beaming.

"Promise to keep it quiet?"

"I promise."

"He did! But you can't tell him. I'm so happy for him. He's such a sweetheart, but he's so shy. I was really worried for him."

"That's so great." I paused, I hoped naturally, and tacked on, "I think I'd like to go on that ER interview."

Becky took a hard look at me. "Five seconds ago you hated blood."

"I was being dramatic. I mean, ironic."

"You were?"

"Are you kidding? The *emergency room*? Becky, what person alive wouldn't want a crack at that! It sounds really cool."

Becky eyed me skeptically. Did she just put two and two together, and remember that Vaughan Nussman was the leading contender for the other slot? "Okay then," she said, and wrote down the interview details. But she wasn't done with her counseling.

"Look, should I call your mom about Out of the Box?"

"How is that internship even allowed?" I said. "Does Dr. Herman really know what her brother does?"

Becky smiled a bit peculiarly and took another sip of her coffee. "Delores seemed a bit embarrassed when she came in with that opening. Something about her brother pressuring her for some cheap, smart help." Becky suddenly realized that once again she was saying way too much for a student to know, and went silent.

I smiled my best smile and said, "Anyhow, I'm grateful for the opportunity to interview at the ER. I promise to report back what it's really like."

"Okay," she said after an exhausted yawn. "But I may send someone else over to Out of the Box if I need to."

So what if Vaughan was a total jerk to me earlier? Now I had a plan to show him up. I mentally tried our coupledom out. Jordie and Vaughan.

6. Allow for Human Error and Move Beyond It

If you find you've made a bad choice of action,
the worst possible thing you can do is give up.
Think hard. Then think again.
Who are your allies? Find someone to
help and make the best of it
(even if it's someone who'll just listen).

The NYU Medical Center emergency room and corridors stank, as you might expect, from medicinal smells. My nostrils were going bonkers, but at least the interview was going perfectly. If I got the spot I would be working with Louise, the very blond chief RN on the floor, who looked to me like she was around my mother's age, forty-fiveish. She had a habit of winking at me whenever she said anything she thought was humorous. "We had a man in yesterday who thought he had ankle cancer. He was absolutely hysterical, and demanded attention. What do you think it was?"

"What?" I said politely.

"A mosquito bite." Wink, wink.

Other than Louise's running commentary on how imperative it was to keep the emergency room sterile, it was ultraquiet in the room the first half hour, and not at all scary.

In fact, the only other sounds were sleeping patients' respirators and loud snoring by a bearded doctor who'd been there all night and fallen asleep on two pushed-together chairs.

I really thought I could handle this internship, even after I caught a strong whiff of someone's number two in a bedpan. So much for the scenes in medical TV shows when all hell breaks loose. In reality, the ER just wasn't that intimidating.

But then things changed for the worse. First a nurse rolled a little redheaded boy with big cheeks right past me. He was motionless and I was horrified. Why wasn't the nurse reacting when it was obvious that he was almost dead?

"He just had his stomach pumped," Louise said when she saw me staring after the boy. "He swallowed some laundry detergent. I'm sure he'll be fine after an hour or so."

I wasn't so convinced. "It's meaningful to work where you can fix things, isn't it?" I said with forced extra enthusiasm to cover my great alarm for the dying kid.

She looked delighted at that comment. "Yes, it is."

I forced out, "I'm convinced it would be an amazing opportunity to work here."

I could tell I was wowing her with my extreme interest in everything she did—fortunately she didn't even ask me about my medical school intent. I could just see Vaughan's jaw drop when the internships were posted on Becky's bulletin board. My whole plan was transpiring flawlessly.

Now flash forward five minutes to when I was barfing as politely as possible (try to picture that) behind an empty hospital bed. I honestly did attempt to get to the ladies' room, but tell me, how often do you see a man's arm hanging on by a thread? A nurse wheeled the incoming patient down to the operating room, and a doctor already checking her bag of scalpels ran behind them. The unexpected eye-gulp of all that arm blood and open flesh (and did I mention the gigantic fresh cut on the patient's forehead?) nauseated me instantly.

Louise was very understanding, considering what a mess I'd made. She promptly had an orderly disinfect the site. "Andre!" she called out to the very unlucky man selected for the task. "Double mop to be sure there is not one dot of the vomit left on the floor!"

Then she finished up with me in her small office. No winking came my way, as she was avoiding any form of eye contact. In fact, she was so busy addressing the elf in the March of Dimes Christmas poster over my head that I knew she would never pick me.

When I arrived home there was a burnt cheesy smell in the air. My father, eastern ad sales director for a Los Angeles film magazine, telecommutes. Dad was so engaged in his TV show that he didn't hear me key in, and I caught him chowing down microwavable enchiladas and watching a *Three's Company* rerun on the newly installed TiVo. Because of our mutual pop culture addiction, Sari always claims I'm Dad's pet. I've always felt that he loves Sari just as much, but her interests perplex him. Dad *always* tunes out when Mom and Sari talk molecules.

Elaine and Ken Popkin are an opposites-attract couple

that has lasted, and Sari is, probably in Dad's mind, his wife's little carbon copy. Mom and Sari are both tall and skinny and delicately pretty even though their light arched eyebrows make them both look a little sad even when they're happy. The only thing Sari has obviously inherited from Dad is his calm nature.

No one questions where I get my looks from either. But genetics are funny: my button nose and my dark lips (not to mention my stubby toes) are just like Dad's, and my size-ten body is very much like the curvy Popkin women's figures I've seen at family bar mitzvahs and weddings. Yet I've been gifted with the Fischer side's tendency to angrily erupt like a volcano.

"What are you doing home?" Dad asked a bit sheepishly as he paused Suzanne Somers in midjiggle around the Ropers' apartment.

I told him the truth about the emergency room. After Dad stopped laughing—the thought of his daughter who wouldn't even get her ears pierced interviewing in a place that's all about blood just struck him as beyond absurd—he agreed I should just go ahead and accept the internship at Out of the Box, which he thought from the sound of it was far, far more suited to me.

He wrote me a note for school and insisted that I not even bother Mom with the fact that I came home without going back to class. Partly, I think, because he didn't want me to mention he was watching nearly pornographic seventies sitcoms while she was hard at work in an office. And especially because cutting a class is major delinquency to Elaine Popkin. She had the perfect attendance record at her high school graduation ceremony, and she doesn't even believe in taking sick days at work.

I was appreciative, but he waved his hand as if to say, *That's nothing.*

"Want to watch TV?" he said.

"Always," I said.

After a commercial for a new spaghetti sauce, an anchorwoman from a daily entertainment gossip program had an exclusive interview with what would be the new mascots for the next winter Olympics in Turin.

"Okay, this is so embarrassing . . . but where's Turin?"

"Italy," Dad said.

"That's where they found a sheet some people think covered Jesus?"

"Yes. Bingo."

We heard a short history of the Olympic mascot, a subject that I'd previously paid zero attention to.

"The first mascot was in 1972, when Munich trotted out Waldi, a multicolored dachshund—"

"Oh, I remember Waldi," Dad laughed to himself. "Bizarre thing."

"But the most famous Olympic mascot was a computer-generated creature who lived in the flame, named Izzy, short for Whatizit? Izzy could transform himself into anything desired."

"Talk about bizarre!" Dad said with another look of glee on his face. "That mascot was unbelievable. He was a computer-generated blob. A marketing disaster."

"In 1988 Calgary, there were Hidy and Howdy, two bears that looked like a cowboy and a cowgirl."

"So hokey!" I said to Dad as I dipped one of Dad's potato chips into his open jar of chunky salsa.

"In 1998 the Nagano mascot was originally a weasel named Snowple, but he was later replaced by the four snow owls, or *snowlets*, named Sukki, Nokki, Lekki, and Tsukki, which all of Japan fell madly in love with."

"Snowlets? They're making this up," I said to Dad.

"The year 2000 in Sydney saw Olly the kookaburra, Millie the echidna, and Syd the platypus."

"Wait, I actually remember that."

"You do?" Dad said. "I don't."

"The most recent ones from Athens were Phevos and Athena, two terra-cotta dolls. The boy doll was named after the Olympian god Apollo, god of light and music, and his sister was named after the goddess of wisdom and patron of the city of Athens."

"I really liked the Athens ceremony," Dad said. "They got it right. First class." He dipped a chip.

"So what will Turin bring?" the coannouncer asked.

I dipped my own chip.

"Two cartoon characters named Neve and Gliz, representing a ball of snow and block of ice, are the cutie-pie mascots for the 2006 Turin Winter Olympics. Neve is red and represents snow, and Gliz is sky blue and symbolizes ice."

Neve and Gliz appeared just then in animated form, right on the set of *Entertainment Daily*, and kissed the hostess.

"I understand you were chosen from more than two hundred entrants."

"Yes," they said in Italian-accented English.

"Well, let me be the first to congratulate you."

"Thank you. We don't speak much English, so *ciao*."

"*Ciao*. See you in Turin."

The animations disappeared.

Dad was still staring at the TV set when he said, "I'm glad I had someone to share that with."

We both burst out laughing at the ridiculousness of it all, and were still cracking up even when the show had moved on to a preview of an "evil chemist" movie called *Bad Science*.

"If the mascots are so embarrassing to people, why do they keep creating them?" I said after a brief exit to the bathroom.

"Licensing moola to be made. Big, big money. Kids love mascots."

"I guess."

"Let me show you my *Syracuse* magazine." Syracuse University is in upstate New York; it's the university my dad attended in the seventies as a double major in marketing and advertising. (*Cough*, Dad was quite the punk rocker, eh?) He reached over and grabbed the glossy publication and shoved the cover photo of a stuffed orange with googly eyes in front of my face.

"That's my mascot. He's at every Orangeman football and basketball game."

"Your school mascot is an orange?"

"After the school color."

"Is he a navel orange?"

Dad laughed. "I'm not sure, but I know originally the

mascot was an Indian warrior, and sometime during the sixties that representation was deemed too derogatory to American Indians."

"Right on." I was big on Native American rights after studying the Trail of Tears the previous year in American history. It was truly shameful that in the mid-1800s the Cherokees were forced to migrate from their land even after a major treaty with the U.S. government was in place.

"I also read in the magazine that no one thought the new mascot would catch on."

He then turned to the middle of *Syracuse*, where they were promoting orange slippers with the mascot face popping up on each foot, and plush twelve-inch orange toys that replicated the mascot. "But just look how many things you can get."

"Hey, I never got a stuffed orange from you."

"Do you want me to order you the sheets with the Orangeman printed on them?" Dad asked, a rhetorical question. He knew how much I loved my floral Laura Ashley sheets I ordered online after I was given the green light by my sister to redecorate Sari-and-Jordie's room as Just-Jordie's room, now that Sari had moved on to dorm life. I was loving my solo bedroom with a Secret Garden theme.

"Next time Boston College plays Syracuse, come upstate with me. You want to see hilarity?"

"Do I!"

"Their eagle mascot runs onto the court after their guys slam dunk, and the crowd boos him, and he shakes his tail feathers at them."

Dad demonstrated by shaking his butt at me.

We heard the door unlocking. Dad rushed to the couch, quickly clicked off the television, and picked up a respectable nonfiction book about the importance of fire in human history—Mom had given it to him for his forty-ninth birthday and had made pointed dinnertime comments about the fact that he never read it.

"Listen," he whispered quickly, "like I told you, I'll handle your mother."

I gave him another grateful hug.

"What a day," Mom said as she plopped into her favorite armchair.

"Hi," I said.

Dad discreetly hid the fatty, nonbaked potato chips my mother still scolds him for eating. "Oh, hi, Elaine."

One of the interesting things my ex–English teacher Mrs. Kleinman often reminded my class was that in real life people hardly ever address each other by their first name. Conversations like that smack of corny old sitcoms.

So when my father said, "Hi, Elaine," his words sounded off.

Mom looked at him funny, like she was going to comment on his odd hello, but then instead she grunted and rose. "Don't think me rude, guys, but I'm starved. I'm starting dinner."

Dad popped up. "You make the salad, Elaine, I'll make the steaks. I checked before, they're all defrosted."

Dad is, by my mother's assessment, a "very progressive" husband, but he still really likes to have dinner served to him. For some reason, Mom tolerates this slightly sexist quirk, especially when he says "pretty please."

"Fine by me," Mom said even more suspiciously.

I have set chores, most of which revolve around the kitchen. I stood up and set the table for three. It was still weird not having Sari at the table.

"So, did you follow up with Dr. Finneran?" Mom said casually as she sliced button mushrooms into the salad bowl.

As I wrestled with what I should say, she looked at me intently and asked, "Is something wrong with your hearing?"

Dad nervously glanced at me from the prep table, where he was rubbing a bit of olive oil onto steaks. He swallowed, slapped the steaks onto the griller, and the PR campaign officially began. "Elaine, I told Jordie that you and I will have a talk about that after dinner, okay?"

Mom looked up and glanced quickly at both of us. She squeezed the garlic press and the inner clove squirted out of its skin. "Oh, is that so?"

She left the internship issue alone for the time being, but I was so anxious that I got a nasty nick on my knuckle when I stupidly grabbed the wrong end of one of the steak knives. A little blob of blood oozed out. But I didn't whine about it. I wanted nothing to distract from the father-daughter battle plan.

Dad has always had this bizarre habit of humming when we eat. You can always tell what's on his mind by the tune he selects. When my sister started dating a Columbia biology grad student who was six years older than her during her last month of high school, Dad got in the habit of humming "I've Got a Right to Sing the Blues."

He claims he's never aware that he's humming, and

Mom usually stops him so she can bring up a dinner conversation she feels is appropriate for family banter, like a new update on our neighbor's ongoing battle with aortic valve trouble or the world's oldest continuously burning lightbulb, which, according to some article she'd read, has inexplicably been shining in a California firehouse for over a hundred years. (Any comment on our favorite reality show gets a frown.)

Mom seemed tired, and after she tonged us all ice cubes for soda glasses, she sat down in silence. I anxiously kept my eyes on my plate and ate and drank quickly even though Dad forgot to put any salt on the steaks. He was soon going to bat for me, so at least I could better the meat without a snide comment. I squeezed the last of the ketchup from a plastic bottle onto my meat. The pressure made an unfortunate noise, but nobody laughed.

Dad's wordless jukebox made it all the way through "It All Depends on You," at which time he leaped up to slice and scoop the seeds out of the melon set aside for dessert. On any other night I would have immediately commented on the runaway cantaloupe seed comically stuck to his chin.

When dinner was over, I rinsed off the dishes and stacked them in the dishwasher in record time. I certainly wasn't going to sit on the couch like some ringside rooter at the big match.

I tried to focus on my precalculus and French assignments, but at one point Mom was yelling so loudly that I was afraid she'd hemorrhage or something. I put on my radio to drown them out. Just after I'd finished my precalculus—I'd been pumping away at my homework so long that the ink in my black ballpoint had come to an end—Dad stuck his head in the door and said, hoarsely from all the fighting, "Mission accomplished. But you better do the dishes for the next year without complaint. And I'm talking scrubbing pad for the pots. No sticking them in the dishwasher and hoping for the best."

I beamed at him. I figured that if advertising was good enough for Dad, Mom could allow me to try it too.

7. Work with Surprises— Expect the Unexpected

Change is all around you.
You may be working on one problem
when another is solved. This is a lucky
surprise. It shows that your creative mind
is working and luck is on your side!
(You might want to hope it stays with you.)

Yes, Mom caved.

My first official day at Out of the Box I promptly walked in around nine a.m. I'd dropped the formal interview wear. My all-black getup of a short denim skirt, crushed velvety top, and flats was nice enough for an office but cool enough to wear to class. This time the receptionist was in place. I had expected a woman. Instead, a man greeted me.

"Hi, I heard about you. I'm Brad." He motioned for my silver North Face parka. "Let me show you the closet. It's hanger heaven in there."

Brad wasn't lying.

There was a rainbow of colored hangers inside the closet. Brad chose one from the pale blue section to hang my coat on.

I thanked him and then he called the premiums extension to let them know their new intern had arrived.

Paulette came to get me a few minutes later. "You look nice," she said. "Way too overdressed for our grubby lot. You can wear ripped jeans tomorrow if you like."

"There she is." Marcus greeted me inside their room.

"Lesson one," Joel said after a big smile. "In advertising you have to think ahead. Anticipate trends."

"Whoa. Maybe she wants some coffee first?" Marcus said.

"Don't get her started on the habit," Paulette replied.

"I'm fine," I chimed in. Five minutes in, I was already a bit overwhelmed by this trio's energy level.

Joel continued, "So, what we're dreaming up here today won't be out for another eighteen months. You have to play chess with your competition, play three moves ahead. What are they thinking? What big tie-in will they sew up? If they have a much cooler movie tie-in, the kids will all clamor for their special meals, and you'll be responsible for pushing a dead product."

"So how do you know what will be in theaters?" I asked.

"Good question," said Marcus. "You check the trades and get as much info from a client as possible."

He put a pile of industry magazines on the table, with *Variety* on top. "Your first task will be to circle anything that has 'kids' or 'family picture' in its description for two Christmases from now."

Over the next half hour as I dutifully did this, my team did nothing but drink coffee and grumble about their boss, the one they called the Pope of Mope.

"He made a fortune from us last year, and I don't see any of that going to us."

"I'll say. A five percent raise? What kind of BS is that?"

"He's so full of it. I heard the Pope presenting one of our ideas to a *Brandweek* reporter the other day. Like he dreamed it up himself."

"Okay, what have you got for us?" Marcus said finally.

I read them the list, which wasn't too long.

"The Eggcups," I said.

"The what?" Paulette said.

"Come again?" Joel said.

I shrugged. "They're eggcups that run around rescuing malnutritioned kids."

"How did that get financed? Even to a creative, that is *bizarre.*"

"And what else?" Joel asked.

"There might be another *Secret Agent Kids* movie."

"Always good. Both genders like the *Secret Agent Kids* franchise. Next?"

"Frogman. That's a comic book adaptation."

"No," Paulette said. "Girls won't like it. Then we have to do a girl companion toy to give to the franchises as a second choice. Twice the work. Twice the expense. They went for it once, but I'm not sure they'd pony up the double manufacturing fees twice in one year."

"Yes," Joel agreed.

"I'll let you in on a little secret," Marcus said. "This presentation to our client must be killer. We've never had much competition. But one of our old staff members has moved to Los Angeles and has started a rival agency. He's right there with the movie studios, and he's got his ear to the ground."

"Another tried-and-true tactic," Paulette added, "is to

tie in to a TV program or an established kids' character. But it's hard to know what is going to stay hot."

Back in French class, I thought about what I had learned that morning.

What I was supposed to be thinking about was French past perfect tense.

I actually had mastered past perfect tense last semester, yet my French teacher, Monsieur Moskowitz, was so wrapped up in his own head that he was teaching it again.

Not that I didn't like or respect Moskowitz very much, I just wished I'd had the foresight to take German with Dr. Zuckendorf, who was supposed to be a fabulous teacher. There weren't many kids who took German, and those who did were a close-knit unit; over two years they'd raised enough money to go to Hamelin, the place where the real Pied Piper piped. And Jeremy's Latin class sounded pretty great—he was always going on about Dr. Horton's hilarious year-end toga parties with eggnog and grape clusters.

It wasn't just me with the wandering mind. Everyone in the class was openly yapping. If a representative of the board of education had dropped by that second, there would definitely have been hell to pay, and I don't think any number of teaching years behind Moskowitz would have saved him.

I eavesdropped a little. "I was reading in *Teen People* that a key sign of depression is overshopping," I overheard Jade Stein say. I liked Jade even though I was hardly a good friend of hers. Jeremy was always talking about what a phony she was, and this was true, in some ways. But she was funny.

One time she confessed to me her plan to make it big in the publishing world: "There's going to be a huge cottage memoir industry when me and my fellow adopted Chinese girls come of age. All the Jade Steins and China Goldsteins and Jasmine Schwartzes are going to flood the market. I'm writing mine now to beat the flood." Funny with a touch of poignancy always scores big points with me.

"How many bags do you have?" said Jade's best friend, a beanpole named Fred who always landed the "zany sidekick" role in our school plays.

"Six."

Fred moaned. "You're a goner. Go directly to therapy."

On the other side of me Clara was telling Blanca and Willie a funny story (she'd already told me outside the class- room) about her internship at the *Times*.

Even though, as I suspected I would be, I was quite bummed that Clara had in fact landed the science journal-ism internship at the *New York Times*, as her best friend I was proud of her too.

Clara could always make me laugh, and the story she was telling the others about the first day of her internship was *hilarious*.

"Then this paid assistant whispered that my boss has a fear of color in her food."

"A fear of color?" Willie checked.

"I didn't get it either. But I checked out what my supervisor was eating for breakfast: egg white omelet and plain yogurt."

"That's not so extreme," Blanca said.

"But what about her lunch, which she also ate at her desk?"

"What did she eat?" Willie said.

Clara leaned forward to whisper loudly, "Steamed white asparagus. Mozzarella. Cauliflower. And white chocolate."

Both Willie and Blanca nearly lost it.

I found myself even more jealous of Clara that day because as usual she was so effortlessly funny. Even now I have to write things down to get any kind of timing. Funny stories just don't come to me that easily when I'm speaking.

Moskowitz clapped his hands to call the many chattering students to attention. "Who is making all of that noise?" he yelled, clueless as ever.

The thirty of us bad sheep were temporarily silenced as Moskowitz slammed shut the classroom door.

84

"I think it is time for French music. There is no better way to learn French than through music."

Moskowitz proceeded to code open a padlock and remove a portable record player from the teacher's locker next to the chalkboard. The record player was dusty and chipped and looked like it was made fifty years ago. Where did that come from? I'd thought I knew all of his teaching gimmicks. He had never brought it out before; in fact, I'd never even seen inside his private cabinet. I couldn't help but notice that in addition to the expected stockpile of textbooks and papers to grade, he had practically a grove of fruit in there too, including, inexplicably, two coconuts.

Clara glanced over at me with a worried expression, and so did Willie.

Then Moskowitz put on Edith Piaf, the mournful French songstress my parents both like.

"*Ecoutez, s'il vous plaît!* You will all be quiet and take in Piaf's glory. Listen hard to her words, and what she is singing."

As we listened to Piaf's voice, my teacher's eyes got wet, but thank God, actual tears did not fall down his cheeks. I was sure I couldn't handle *that*.

The afternoon was turning out strange but kind of cool. This woman could sing. Beautifully.

Then—and no one saw this coming—Moskowitz started to sing too!

"*Non, je ne regrette rien . . .*"

His voice was not half bad. Deep and baritoney.

I quickly translated Edith Piaf's/Mr. Moskowitz's words in my head as *No, I have no regrets*.

As Moskowitz wiped his damp eyes, my class fought back titters.

The thing was, I found my French teacher singing sad love songs surprisingly comforting, and I was soon caught up in my own thoughts again.

I wondered how Vaughan had done on his first day at the emergency room. I was sure he wouldn't barf at dangling limbs.

I looked around the class and saw Zane all the way on the other side of the room. He was in both of my afternoon classes. He caught my eye and smiled at me.

He pointed to Moskowitz and with a grin put an imaginary pistol to his own temple, squinted, and pulled the trigger.

Afterward the whole class was gathered outside the door, trying to make sense of what we had just witnessed.

"What does one say after that experience?" Blanca said.

"One doesn't," Clara said.

"He's just so pathetic that I can't find it in myself to ridicule him," Willie said.

"You know, his voice isn't so bad," Blanca said.

I nodded. "I was getting into the whole thing."

Clara peered at Blanca and me with some form of emotion . . . disgust? "You two are unreal." But her eyes gave her away. She was as seriously amused as us.

Zane was standing near me, and coughed uncomfortably. "How's your internship?" he managed to ask after the hallway thinned out.

"It's a little unusual," I admitted.

"Where did you get placed?"

"Promise not to tell?"

"Sure, if that's important to you."

"They're an ad agency."

"Why is that so embarrassing?"

"I just don't want to hear from Vaughan how I sold out."

"You care that much about what Vaughan thinks?"

"Well, it's a little more extreme than just an ad agency."

"What, they hype guns?"

"They sell fast-food toys. They're a premium agency."

"You mean like Happy Boxes?"

"Yes."

"That's where you're interning? I thought you had to have a science internship."

"There's an odd connection to Dr. D."

"Which is?"

"One of my bosses is her brother."

"How many bosses do you have?"

"Three. All wacky but nice. I'm a little embarrassed that I'm not saving lives—"

"Well, at least what you experience should be interesting."

I smiled at him. "That it is." Then I remembered to ask, "How's yours?"

"Amazing."

"Yeah, my sister loved it there too."

"Your sister," Zane said dramatically.

"My sister what?"

"Sari Popkin is all I hear about in the department. It's kind of tough there. I hope I can live up to her standards."

The bell rang for the next class, and Zane had to go. He had a ninth period class.

I, however, was done for the day, and headed toward the subway. School was three stops from my apartment. (My parents let me take the subway by myself. Subways are speedy.)

I was thinking about Moskowitz singing and for some reason started to think of my internship and how some premiums could come with singing voices.

Which characters?

How about presidents? What would be funny for presidents to sing?

Too dopey, I told myself. They'd have to license the music too, so it would probably be too expensive to be worth making.

I tried to think of the Burger Man Happy Box toys I liked as a kid: my favorite cartoon characters on skateboards.

Why not put those newly announced cute mascots in Olympic poses? You wouldn't have to pay any music rights. And why wouldn't the Olympics marketing people love to get invaluable exposure with American youth?

Even though I was excited by this idea, I decided to keep it to myself. I was a sixteen-year-old who had been in the room with marketing geniuses for exactly four hours.

8. Brainstorming: Make It a Way of Life

Always be thinking—
inside or outside the box.
(Some of the world's greatest
inventions came from silly ideas.)

"There she is!" genius Marcus called out when I walked in.

"Day two!" genius Joel said.

"This is actually a very important day for us," genius Paulette said.

"How's that?" I asked.

"We're having a little visit from the Burger Man man at noon," Marcus said.

"Burger Man woman," Paulette corrected.

Marcus looked at Paulette. "Woman? Do you think John would like to know you're calling him a woman?"

"John was fired," Joel said.

Marcus seriously whitened at the news. "What? Was anyone going to tell me this?"

"I forgot. I just got a call from her."

"Her?"

"The new woman."

"Well, that's just great. It took me a year to figure out John's peccadilloes, and now there's some lady—"

"I don't think she has the same position as John. I think John's boss is now handling the decisions, and she's just giving him a report. That's what I picked up from what she said."

"John's boss? John's boss is Victor Cohen. Humorless."

They soon forgot all about me again. I hung up my coat. No, no way would I bring up my big Olympics mascot brainstorm. Marcus angrily sifted through the contents of his in-box. Then, out of the blue, he sniffed the air. "Do you smell something bad?"

Paulette kept working on her computer. There was so much tension in the air that I could not imagine how everyone was going to get through this morning.

"Listen, I showered," Joel said finally. "Maybe there's a bit of my liverwurst sandwich from yesterday left over?"

"You eat liverwurst voluntarily?" I asked.

"Not just any liverwurst sandwiches, my friend," Joel said. "These are Linus Loves Liverwurst sandwiches from *The Charlie Brown Cookbook*. So extra special."

Marcus's tone was back to jokey. "Joel's a soft touch for anything to do with Linus. Hence the blankie."

I looked where he was pointing. There was a holey baby blue blanket on top of the filing cabinet that somehow I'd missed seeing before.

Paulette said, "I don't smell anything. Ever since your sinus infection your senses are going crazy with phantom odor."

"Crazy? I actually think my olfactory nerves are more

sensitive," Marcus said. As he stood, he pretended to be a bloodhound sniffing around the room, picking up the scent. "I'm hot on the trail."

Joel pulled a face. "That's the best you can do as a dog? We're teaching the next generation here."

He crouched to the floor, and Marcus and Joel circled each other, woofing and yipping.

"Come on, Paulette, show us what a dog you are."

Paulette was not moving. She reached into a drawer full of unraveled Slinkys and other playthings and grabbed an open tube of kids' Pick Up Sticks. She fished out a yellow one and pushed some of her cuticles back. She looked up, acted surprised that we were all waiting for her answer, and finally said, simply, "Bark."

"We're trying to relax here after the bad news. So of course Her Highness is not taking part in this. . . ." I was growing weary of the rapid-fire mood swings all around me; now Marcus's voice sounded annoyed again.

"I'm a pampered pooch."

He rolled his eyes.

"Enough," she said to him. "I am bored witless with your tantrums, but even more so with the daily playacting. It was cute when I started here, but not after the five millionth time."

"And you, Miss Intern?" Marcus said to me. "Are you also too highfalutin to be a dog?"

"Are you going to snap a leash on me if I bend down?"

Paulette snorted at my crack.

"No," Marcus promised after his own grin.

I dropped to the floor. I'm glad none of my friends could

see me as I coughed and barked. Rather than be embarrassed for me, as Jeremy and Clara would surely be, Marcus and Joel reacted like crouching and barking was the only thing I *should* do.

Marcus pawed a filing cabinet. "I think I found the culprit."

He stood up and grabbed a vase of wilted, molding yellow roses.

"Since you are our intern, you must smell for us."

Joel and Paulette laughed together this time. I stood up a bit angrily.

"It's true," Joel said. "Your first days here are intern initiation days. When I started at my first ad agency, I had to scrub three baked lasagna pans in my first week."

Again, I didn't want to be a spoilsport, so I obeyed. "Gross—rotten flower water," I said, sickened by the stench and more than annoyed about this just-revealed hierarchy.

"Who's in charge of flowers here?" Joel asked. "The scent of old flower water is the worst smell in the world, is it not?"

"RIP, little roses," Paulette said. "They were beautiful once. I got those at the Union Square farmers' market."

"When?" Joel said sarcastically.

"Sorry, guys—last month."

"Righto," Joel said. "Second task, Jordie. Clean up the manky flower water."

The fake lingering smile on my face disappeared. If this was what I was going to do here, I wanted out. When I returned from the lobby, my hands stank so badly that I went directly to the bathroom sink.

I washed my hands with cherry soap, angry as anything.

Back in the premium section, nobody was a dog any-more.

There was a flip chart out, and there were three terms already up on the board: *Bubble Gum. Peppermint. Chocolate Brownies.*

"We're having a big groupthink about scents," Marcus informed me. No one even thanked me for cleaning out the vase. "We've decided that with a new person on the scene, we better come up with backup ideas. Can you add one?"

"Cherry soap," I said sharply.

"Think premiums, kid."

"I don't know. . . ." This was my second day! I'd confidently walked in with what was, in my mind, the premium idea of the century, and now I'd been given my proper place, and my hands stank of gross flower water! I was not a happy camper.

"Try another fruit."

"Strawberries," I said quietly. "Strawberry Shortcake."

"Excellent idea," Joel said. "Girls love her."

"That's true," Paulette said. "That was a good idea."

Marcus was not as impressed. "Nice, but didn't McDonald's do that for Happy Meals in 2001?"

"Not sure." Joel looked at me and commanded, "Write that down and look into it for us when we're done here."

"Write what down?"

"I'll write it down for you," Joel said as he reached for a four-by-six index card. He added out loud, "Strawberry Shortcake. McDonald's. 2001?"

"Skunks," Joel said to Marcus as he handed me the index card.

"Pepé Le Pew," Marcus rallied. "Little wind-up Pepé Le Pew skunks that stink when you scratch their bellies."

"You'd have to be a kid born in 1945," Joel scoffed. "Our target market doesn't even remember the Teenage Mutant Ninja Turtles."

"Most of them weren't even born," Paulette agreed, and then added, "Roses. Gardenias."

"Pinecones," I said loudly, surprising myself.

After that I'm not sure who was calling out what. It sounded like we were in a frantic auction.

"Lime Jell-O."

"Coca-Cola."

"Eucalyptus."

"Coppertone suntan oil."

"Aftershave? Nothing stinks more than my father's aftershave."

"Always popular with the under-four set desiring Happy Boxes."

"Tacos."

"Apple pectin."

"Ooh, I love apple shampoo," Paulette said. "The best shampoo, though, was Body on Tap. A beer shampoo in the seventies."

I had no idea what she was talking about. A beer shampoo?

"Coffee."

"That's not a scent for a three-year-old—"

"Lemon."

"Good for your dishwashing liquid, not for a premium."

"Vinegar."

"Who wants to smell vinegar?"

"I don't know. Kids like disgusting things."

"How about fish, then?"

"Mowed grass."

"Marijuana," Joel said.

"Shut up, wiseass," Marcus said back.

"No censoring, remember?" Joel barked.

"Bad breath."

"Gasoline."

"Pickle."

"Garlic."

"Horse manure."

"You know what?" Joel said. "I used to have those scratch and sniff stickers when I was a kid. Why don't we bring that back? Do foul smells. Kids *love* foul smells."

Paulette clapped her hands. "People. People. Foul smells don't sell hamburgers. The people who buy hamburgers the most are churchgoing folk."

And then, just as quickly as the mayhem started, it stopped.

"Okay, that was good," Marcus said. "Time for lunch."

I looked at the clock. It wasn't even ten-thirty in the morning, but he opened up a Three Stooges lunch box and out came an overstuffed New York deli corned beef sandwich, a pickle, and a diet root beer.

"So, what's the premium going to be?" I said, having calmed down internally.

"What?" Marcus said after he'd swallowed his first chew of meat.

"All that work for nothing?"

"That? That *was* nothing."

97

"So." Joel broke into our conversation. "What will you do when you leave us at one o'clock?"

"I have classes."

"What classes? I've blotted out everything from my high school years."

"I don't have a full load because of my internship. But I have French and precalculus."

"Boyfriend?" Paulette asked.

"No, not at the moment."

"Is there a guy you like?" Paulette followed up.

"Maybe." I was a little uncomfortable with this sudden attention.

"What's his name?"

"His name is Vaughan." I lingered a little too long over his name and reddened slightly.

Marcus made a knowing face. "Did you hear the way she said his name? She fancies the pants off him."

"Is *Vaughan* in your French class?" Joel said.

"Actually, he's in my precalculus class. The God of Room 207."

"I'll tell you how to get *Vaughan*," Marcus said.

"I'd love to hear it," I said. Glad to see my life was a joke to these people.

"Feed him milk."

Excuse me? Was I the butt of somebody's joke here?

Joel laughed out loud, but Paulette rolled her eyes.

"What did you do over the weekend, have a lobotomy?" she said. "I have to pee badly. When I get back, hopefully you'll have moved on, stupid man."

"Don't be such a sourpuss, dollface," Marcus said to her.

"I read in this book once that man always unconsciously thinks back to his original love, his mother. Mommy and milk; what could be better than bathing a man in nostalgic emotions? You've got to trigger that emotion subliminally, though. Did you ever hear about the liquor ad where they spelled out 'sex' in the ice cubes?"

"First you offer her coffee," Joel said as he paused to laugh, "and now—don't drag in the subliminal sex ice cube spiel. Let her hear all about that in her college marketing classes."

Paulette stood by to hear the idea burst. "So she should feed him ice cream?" she prodded.

"Yes," Marcus said sheepishly. "Or she could 'inadvertently' brush the God's elbow and use that as an opportunity to chat him up and offer him a milk shake."

Needless to say, there was a big fat zero chance of my following his tip.

"File it away," Paulette said, seconding my thoughts, "under moronic suggestions."

She then raced for the ladies' room a few feet away.

With his teeth Joel ripped open a vacuum-packed foil pouch of no-drain tuna fish. "See this?" he said to me. "This is true innovation. I rank this just behind the guy who came up with the idea of launching the space shuttle on a piggyback ride with a Boeing 747. Who wants to cart around a can opener?"

"Not me," I agreed.

"Ruffled her feathers," Marcus said out of the blue. "You've probably already noticed that everything is wrong to Paulette." He coughed suddenly as Paulette walked back into the room.

"Are you going to wire me up next, tell me what to say that in your opinion is right?"

"Not a bad idea."

"God! You're still such a control freak—"

Marcus stood up and caught her elbow. "Lower your foghorn, will you, Paulette?"

Paulette twisted away and sat in her chair.

Suddenly this workday was getting pretty hairy. My friends at school got worked up over minor stuff, but I wasn't used to dealing with this kind of emotion from adults. So what happened here? Had they had a thing?

"Your daily pokes at me are about as entertaining as a bassoon solo," she said. Which was a strange thing to say.

Apparently, I was not the only one who thought this.

"Did you know that Paulette is newly enrolled in a comedy improv class?" Marcus asked Joel.

"I didn't know that," Joel said.

"Marcus, that was a private fact!" Paulette replied.

Marcus didn't apologize. "If you are working on your comedy, may I suggest that a handbell solo is a much funnier choice of words?"

"Not only are you a chronic gossiper, but you always have to have the last word. Ugly."

"He's right, you know," Joel said after a few tension-filled seconds. "Handbells are much funnier than bassoons."

"Quick, neutral party," Marcus said to me. "Which is funnier, bassoon solo or handbell solo?"

"Handbell solo," I answered guiltily. I just had to. It *was* a funnier word choice.

There was a teeny smile on Paulette's face.

Marcus abruptly stopped his warring, took a penny out of his pocket, and slammed it in front of Joel and his tuna-chunk sandwich. "A penny for your thoughts."

Joel took the penny, and another forkful of tuna went into his mouth. He looked at Marcus and said, "In a world in which the human mind can be programmed like a computer, where does the human soul end and the cybernetic machinery begin?"

"Here," Marcus said drily, extending his arm, "give the freaking penny back."

After his tuna was done, Joel beckoned me with a finger. "Come. Follow me."

He led me down a carpeted hallway to a room full of dozens of hobby books with memorable names like *Pictorial Price Guide to Vinyl & Plastic Lunch Boxes & Thermoses*, *The Big Bible of Peanut Butter and Jam Glasses*, *Hot Wheels: The Recent Years*, and *Toys That Shoot*.

He pulled a fat paperback book off the shelf. "This is the most valuable book in our library. Anyone who removes it from here gets shot by Brad the receptionist."

"What is it?"

"*Kovels'*. The bible for anyone who makes premiums for a living. If you read carefully, you'll be able to track down the last time Strawberry Shortcake was used as a premium, if ever. When you're finished I have some filing for you."

It looked like Marcus was right about the premium. A Strawberry Shortcake premium was done within the last two years.

While I had the *Kovels'* collectibles guidebook out, I snuck a look at the value of my old Cinderella Timex watch

I had when I was around six years old. Worth about thirty bucks. And Mom wanted me to toss it!

I had plenty of experience filing during my summer job at my mother's office. Filing is as enjoyable as pulling clumps of matted wool off an old sweater, but I was guessing that despite the stinky flower water incident, I had it good for the Manhattan Science interns. I could more than deal with half my "duties" being seriously fun.

Soon enough, it was noon. When the receptionist called Paulette's line, she asked me to go bring in the rep. "Her name is Daisy," she told me.

"Daisy?" Marcus wrinkled his nose.

She stared at him. "Hush now, idiot, your big fat voice carries."

I went to the reception couches.

There was a very beautiful blond woman sitting down with her legs crossed. *Dressed to the nines*, as Grandma Pearl says.

"Are you Paulette?" she asked.

"Oh no, I'm the intern," I said. "Can I show you the way?" I'd seen just enough movies that I knew I should say something professional like that.

"Welcome, welcome." Marcus took her through the Burger Man presentation, which meant everything they had talked about to me before, including the tie-in to the *Eggcups* movie. Nothing from our crazy morning brainstorming session was brought up. Maybe that insanity was just a warm-up exercise for them.

Daisy spoke in a monotone, but only from time to time.

She had less personality than a statue of a Russian despot. Marcus was talking strangely during the meeting, even for him. Maybe the switcheroo of executives was the cause, but I suspected it was because both Daisy's preppy pink twinset and straight black skirt were so tight and revealing. She was also wearing shiny stockings, the pricey kind Mom buys from Bloomingdale's for weddings.

"Victor asked me to remind you of the value of bankability," she said at one point.

"Yes, of course," Marcus said automatically.

"Anyone can give you bankability," Joel cut in.

Marcus, alarmed, continued his pitch. "What you need is creativity and a smart team. Everyone knows that the inducement for the parent to get a toy with a meal is a few minutes of peaceful eating. But just cranking out anything tying in to a current movie is a shortsighted approach. Because the kids are your word-of-mouth sellers here, and no kid is going to tell his or her friends to go to Burger Man if the toy is dull to play with. Our toys are timely *and* fun. That's what differentiates our approach."

I wrote the word *bankability* in that spiral notebook I was keeping for my semester-end report.

The woman looked at me curiously when I put the pen on my pad. "Why are you actually in this room, by the way? I thought you said you are the intern."

I coughed uncomfortably.

Paulette spoke for the first time before I could respond. "She's learning all about marketing for high school credit."

"Has she signed a confidentiality contract?" Daisy asked sternly.

"What?" Paulette said.

"At Burger Man, we have all our temps and interns sign a confidentiality clause."

"We have a better method," Marcus said.

"What's that?" she asked.

Yes. What was he talking about?

"Jordie, can you look at me for a second?"

I did.

"If you ever give these ideas to the competition, do you know what will happen?"

"What?"

"I'll *moider* you!" He said that exactly like Moe from the Three Stooges.

I laughed. "Understood."

Paulette laughed.

Joel laughed.

Daisy, however, had a blank look on her face. "So, when do you think you can get it to us?" she said finally.

"Monday."

"Good. If you are doing anything too outlandish, change the calculus. By the way, is there a funny odor in here?"

"Wash those hands again," Paulette whispered to me on the way out.

"She was incredibly smart," Marcus said after the bland woman left.

"I sure hope that was a joke," Joel said immediately.

"Why, because she said the word 'calculus'?" Paulette chimed in. "You could tell she was just repeating what her boss was saying to her. Otherwise she just nodded at everything you said, even when you were talking utter garbage."

"That's why he thinks she's so smart," Joel cracked.

Marcus smirked. "Could it be that our Paulette is threatened by another talented woman on the scene?"

"Idiot," Paulette muttered not so quietly.

Marcus continued, "You'd be shocked, Jordie, but our Paulette has a lovely figure. I don't know why she hides it from the world."

"No one's hiding anything!"

Marcus gave Paulette's outfit a long look and then gave Joel a really mean smile. I hated him slightly for being so awful to Paulette, but I had to agree with him about her lack of caring. Paulette had on an unflattering winking dog sweatshirt, another pair of vintage Levi's that were ratty, and on her feet a pair of cutesy socks with little hearts all over them. It was as if she was wearing exactly what she'd worn to junior high years earlier.

105

"Why are you so happy when you insult me?" Paulette said finally.

"I think he was flattering you," Joel said.

"Both of you, leave," Paulette said with a snap-to-it voice. "Go to lunch at the coffee shop. I have real work to do."

"I bought my lunch," Joel protested.

"Whadja buy?" Marcus asked.

"Minestrone soup from the deli—"

Paulette sliced the air with an arm. "I said leave."

My assigned task for the remaining thirty minutes of my internship day was to try my hand at writing a summary of the meeting. I sat in front of a computer and tried my best. At one point the phone rang, and Paulette cut the caller off with a quick "No, *tomorrow* it'll be ready."

After she hung up we said nothing for the longest while, but I could tell when I stretched out for a second that she was still mulling over Marcus's comments. She was just sitting there with such an agonized expression I almost wanted to hug her.

"Do you agree with him?" she said unexpectedly.

"Marcus? I don't think it's my place to give you a critique."

"You have permission. I think a lot of people are thinking things around here and not telling me what they are really thinking."

She sounded a bit lunatic when she addressed me. Another expression my grandmother says popped into my head: her voice was *unbuttoned*.

I sighed. By mentioning her appearance so heartlessly, Marcus had dropped a bomb and left others to deal with the consequences.

"Oh boy, is it that bad?" she said at my nonanswer.

"You look like you're in nice shape to me."

Her face brightened. "Both of my parents are ectomorphs—the naturally skinny body type. I'm lucky there."

"I'm sure when you decide to dress up nicely, you'll look great."

She winced.

That didn't exactly come out the way I wanted it to, but I'd said enough.

She reached over to Joel's desk for his vintage bicycle bell and flicked it with her thumb until it made its noise.

"She was an office flunky sent to spy on us," she said a minute or two later. "She wasn't a creative at all."

Joel and Marcus returned shortly.

"I'm sorry if I offended you," Marcus said. "You egged me on."

"Don't worry about it," Paulette said, as if he should worry. She handed Joel back his bicycle bell and everyone silently went back to work, except me. It was time to go back to school, and the God of Room 207.

9. Take Risks

Are you up for true experimentation?
Those willing to go out on the longest
limb have often been rewarded with
tremendous success. The creative who
combined peanut butter and jelly in one
jar may have been mocked by friends,
but he or she is laughing
all the way to the bank.

The subway train was mercifully right there when I got to the station. I looked at my watch when I was about a block away from school: I was over thirty minutes early for pre-calculus. There was no traffic, so as I crossed the last street, I looked up, something I rarely do. I'd never noticed the words chiseled in the long capstone above my high school before. Words attributed to Albert Einstein: IMAGINATION IS MORE IMPORTANT THAN KNOWLEDGE. I stopped walking and retreated a bit. I sat on that brownstone stoop across the street from school that my little gang favored, and for a minute or so I thought about Einstein's advice.

I wondered what Marcus, Joel, and Paulette would have been like in high school.

I bet Joel was hilarious in those days, but he probably got picked on.

Marcus could have been a chronic overachiever. Imagine having his sister as sibling competition, though. I had a lot of issues with my sister, but she was overall a nice person, unlike Dr. D.

And Paulette? What on earth was she like? Did she have that awful frizzy hair in school? That shocking fashion sense? I sure hoped Paulette's dry, funny cracks made her popular despite her offbeat looks. Her comments reminded me of that writer Dorothy Parker, who Mrs. Kleinman told us about in her class. I did a report on her life after Kleinman's brief introduction. Dorothy Parker was a depressed person, but she always had a sharp comment to make. And it wasn't just her one-liners like "Men seldom make passes at girls who wear glasses" that were really funny. "The Waltz," the short story we had to read by her, was so wonderfully written and so, so funny. Or as my teacher put it, "jaunty stuff." I bet Dorothy Parker would have been awesome to have as a friend in school.

I laughed to myself about Marcus and the stupid milk theory.

But just to be on the safe side, I took a detour to a Burger Man a block from school to buy two vanilla milk shakes. I would never admit it to Marcus, but when it came to Vaughan, I was willing to try anything to get him to appreciate me.

As I was second in line the little kid in front of me begged his mother to get him a Happy Box.

"A Happy Box? Oh, honey, those things are so babyish. You're a big kid now."

"I want it, Mommy. I want it. I only have the hand buzzer and the flower squirter."

"How did you even get those?"

"Daddy always gets me a Happy Box!"

The mother groaned and ordered a Happy Box.

Field research I could give to my supervisors. The premiums worked. But did they really need to hear that? They wouldn't have a job if it didn't work. People like Vaughan would say I was part of the system. Corrupting youth. I was sure he wouldn't see an iota of worth in what I was doing.

Was there any?

Those disturbing thoughts were poking in my brain again, but it was a little too late to do some real doubting. Was advertising to kids really where my creative energy should go? I wondered if that was why Paulette asked me if I was morally opposed to what they did. Maybe she had wrestled with this dilemma herself. Maybe she had wanted to be a journalist once and hated that her bills were paid this way.

When they installed an electronic scoreboard with a Burger Man logo in our auditorium, I had accepted that as the way things are.

"Two vanilla milk shakes," I said softly when it was my turn.

Whatever the morality of the premiums business, I wasn't the one to fix it in an afternoon. Right now, I just wanted to see if Marcus's milk tip would work with Vaughan.

My high school had an elaborate security "gun and knife" checkpoint you needed to clear to get past the door. That's another reality of a New York public school—even though the crimes more likely to be committed inside the sacred walls of Manhattan Science were of the cheating kind. I had to show my student ID even though the guards had seen me come in and out of the building for two years. Dr. D wasn't taking any risks after a shocking gun death at a nearby public high school of high repute.

Even with my stop for the milk shakes, even with the ID check, I was the first one in the precalculus classroom. Mr. Etchingham wasn't even in the room yet.

"Hi," I said when Vaughan entered room 207. He must have been coming directly from his ER internship. He was so achishly a hottie that I flinched a bit.

"Hey, how's it going?" he responded nonchalantly.

"Good. How's your internship going?"

"I got off early today, but I can see it's going to be really challenging. But rewarding."

"Are there two of you there?"

"How did you know that?"

"Oh, I just heard." I hesitated for moment and added, "So, who is the other intern?" I felt a little queasy in anticipation as I asked that.

"Robert Mitchelson."

Good, good, good. Not a girl.

"Hey, you want a milk shake?"

I was hoping to be *jaunty* like Dorothy Parker, but my "irreverent" statement got no smile out of him, just a confused look.

"A milk shake," I repeated. "From Burger Man. I have an extra one."

"Why do you have an extra milk shake?"

"Well, this girl I know works at Burger Man as a supervisor, and she ran out and gave me two when she saw me passing by the window."

"Okay," he said, and he looked amused as I pulled the shakes from my bag and leaned toward him with one in the most seductive way I could without giving away my greater scheme. "Thanks," he said a bit uneasily, like the next thing I was going to say was that I enjoyed kicking tin cans for fun.

He continued to drink my "love offering" even as our fellow classmates scrambled in and finished the last of their between-classes sodas and corn chips. But then Etchingham pushed through the door, and in a pleasant voice he'd never used addressing me, asked Vaughan to trash it. Vaughan winked at me as the empty cup went into the bin, and I am sure both Jeremy and Zane noticed that, because they looked at both of us again quickly, especially when I quietly got up and threw a half-empty milk shake in the trash can too.

"By the way," Vaughan said. "Does something in that trash stink?"

"There's some rotting fruit in there," I lied, and hid my hands behind my back.

"Oh, *that's* it."

Of course after precalculus I washed my hands about five times before heading to French class.

This afternoon Moskowitz decided not to break out the portable player. For some reason, perhaps out of pity after his concert, my class behaved better, silently listening as he finally hit us with new study material. The only extra noise in the room this time was from the rattly radiator.

Since I planned on taking my New York State French Regents Exam the next term, a statewide test whose results were reported to colleges, I obediently wrote down his list of ten French adverbs. Moskowitz's handwriting, like his personality, was tilted. The last parts of his words rose several inches above the first few letters.

happily . . . *gaiment*
shyly . . . *timidement*
softly . . . *doucement*
carefully . . . *attentivement*
neatly . . . *proprement*
weakly . . . *faiblement*
easily . . . *facilement*
first . . . *premièrement*
now . . . *maintenant*
never . . . *jamais*

It was dulldom as usual. Clara passed me a note: *What is that awful smell in here?*

"So, what did you do in your new internship today?" my father asked when I got home.

"We were brainstorming premium ideas."

You could hear my mom's scoff from the sink as she sprinkled salt and pepper on our pork loins. She was home early after having an iffy stomach. Was that really it? How could it be iffy if she was cooking pork? And remember, she *never* took sick days.

"I just can't imagine that it would be so hard to do that they need a team," my mother said.

Dad turned toward me with an apologetic expression.

"Mom, these are *professional* brainstormers," I tried again.

Dad coughed loudly.

"What did your work entail?" she said a bit more agreeably.

"We were thinking about different scents that kids like."

"That sounds fascinating," my father said. He caught sight of my mother's barely hidden grimace. "Doesn't that sound great?"

"Fascinating," Mom said with great effort.

"Mom," I directly challenged her, "do you even believe that what I'm doing during the day is stimulating my brain?"

"Nearly," she said softly as she portioned off a serving to cook for each of us.

Nearly? What the hell was that supposed to mean?

While she was lining the bottom of our stove with tin foil, she said, "So, I heard from Sari. She's doing nicely."

"Good," Dad said.

"She's getting close to committing to her thesis."

"What's she thinking of?"

"The luminosity of the lanterneye fish."

"Oh," Dad said.

"Oh," I said.

"A lot of research has been done on the fish, but not too many people have taken a closer look at the phosphorescent bacteria that form in the fish's luminosity organ."

Dad kicked me under the table to be sure I wouldn't snicker.

"She has to be so careful because as a scientist, even an undergraduate, when you commit, it could be your life's work."

"Of course," Dad said.

Actually, I was more annoyed than amused. It was always the same pattern. I would bring something up about my day and she would bring something up about my sister's day. I wondered if she ever sang my praises to my sister when I wasn't around. I suspected not.

"I'm glad Sari's getting so close." Dad scrunched his nose and added, "Does something stink?"

"Something *is* a little foul," Mom agreed. "Could it be a moldy towel somewhere?"

"I think it's your hands," Dad said.

"My hands?" Mom said.

"Jordie's."

"Still? I had to change the dirty flower water, but I've been washing all—"

"For crying out loud. They have my daughter changing flower water?"

It was my turn to clean up after dinner, but they both *insisted* I take a bath.

A bath rather than a shower was my favorite thing now,

especially since my sister's departure. Sari's favorite habit besides using my mascara—she was the scientist with training wheels on, didn't she know that sharing mascara breeds germs?—was the forty-five-minute shower. As I've said, except for her calm temperament, she's scarily like my mother. Now our shared bathroom was all mine, mine, mine.

I removed several rose-scented candles from my bath box I kept in the closet of my room. And poured in my trusty bubble bath. I still like the comfort of the pink Mr. Bubble packaging. With my tubful of suds I pretended to be a Hollywood starlet in a glamorous sunken tub. "It all started," I said to an imaginary interviewer, "when I met these three crazy ad people. . . ."

Mom may have hated my new situation, but I was thrilled to be on my way. Exactly where I was going, I wasn't sure, but since meeting the three maniacs at Out of the Box, I really did feel the thrust of motion in my life.

I clicked open the bathroom door when I was done. I was wrapped in the white Turkish terry robe I'd gotten for Hanukkah, and wearing one of Mom's many bath turbans. I was just about to open my bedroom door and change into my sushi-print pajamas when I heard my father say, "How did you get along with Martin today?"

Martin was my mother's new boss. I met him when I worked for her office the summer before. He struck me as dull as sawdust, but she never really talked about him to me.

My mother's voice was noticeably unsteady when she answered him. "*Such* a pain. He wants printouts of my e-mails, so I give them to him."

"E-mails!" Dad cried.

"And he calls me in and says he doesn't like diagonal staples. He is a man who 'likes neat, horizontal stapling.' "

"That's insanity. After you turned around that comet book in a month? You said Dana said it was a bang-up job."

Dana is the president of my mother's publishing company.

"I'm not kidding. He was eating carrots at the same time, and little orange bits were all over his teeth—I think Bugs Bunny is out to get me. I was so depressed about it I had to leave early."

I didn't think that was so funny, but my father did. "Bugs! That's exactly who he looks like." His laughter leveled off. "Listen, you keep perfect records. You haven't had anything but positive evaluations. You are a meticulous woman with a gift for introducing hard concepts to young kids. No one's going to touch you."

"You always back me up, honey. I love you for that."

"If Bugs goes after you, I'll make rabbit stew out of him."

I was shocked that Mom had any trouble on the job. But it was comforting to hear my parents' connection. It amazed me once again how much my very different parents clicked.

There's a little ledge in the hallway, between our apartment's two bedrooms, where my mom has framed various family photos, including a slew of ancestors who expired eons before I was delivered exactly at noon uptown in a Mount Sinai Hospital delivery room. One I've always been drawn to is of my mother's grandmother when she was a young girl with ringlets. In this picture she is sitting on a small slatted chair on a grassy field, and her feet are bare and

little dirty. She is smiling big. Mom say some town on the Polish-Russian border.

Could my great-grandmother Yetta l brained person too?

Was my Olympic mascot idea anything ad people would appreciate? Was I a creati a capital C? I wrote a big note about my i second notebook.

At least from the meeting I knew D hadn't chosen a premium yet. What if he to them for more ideas? The Olympics There was bankability in it, wasn't there? possibility they'd fall in love with my idea

10. Sexiness Sells

What's sexy? Figure this out from your point
of view and from his. Get a whitening
toothpaste. Make sure you wash your
face in the morning, and put on a clean shirt.
If you think people don't notice
small details, think again.
Spruce yourself up a bit. A low-cut
shirt is okay, but don't get too slutty!
A hint of what's inside is more enticing.
Remember, you are the package.
Would you want what you see?

Paulette waved from behind her computer screen. Marcus, standing over her, gave me a silly grin for his morning hello. As they seemed busy with a project, I simply said hello and got to work with the filing pile. It wasn't too bad, about ten minutes' worth, and then I would be done and wait for my next instructions for the day. There was a nice smell in the area, and I was slightly shocked to realize that it came from Paulette. She hadn't worn perfume the other times I'd been around her. I looked at her briefly, but she was still clicking, with Marcus watching not directly over her shoulder, but nearby. Something else about Paulette was different that I just couldn't figure out yet.

"The B-52's played in New York?" Marcus asked Paulette. "Are they still alive?"

Maybe they weren't so busy.

"Don't read it!" Paulette shrieked. How did she even

know that Marcus was reading what she was scrolling? Sometimes Paulette was like a housefly, with eyes that could see all around.

"What's your problem?" Marcus yelled right back.

Paulette kept scrolling along. "You're going to finish the damn review before me, and then start commenting on it. You know they're still my favorite band, so stop it! That's like opening a gift before the recipient."

"You are the most hypersensitive—"

Joel walked in with a can of peach soda. I shook my head to warn him of the tension in the room.

"So any word from Burger Man?" My meek attempt to diffuse the tension.

Joel shook his head. "Nothing. Nada. We're waiting it out."

"So, what would you like me to do today after I finish filing?"

"Why don't we just focus on *you*," Joel said.

"Me?"

Joel eyeballed me. "How's it coming with lover boy?"

I smiled and said, "Actually, I was early for the class we share—seventh-period precalculus—and I was buying myself some food and, well, I gave him Marcus's suggested milk shake."

Even Paulette looked up.

"Really!" Marcus said. "And?"

"What happened?" Joel asked.

"Well, he took it. But he looked at me like I was an idiot."

"Should have listened to me," Paulette muttered.

Suddenly, I knew what was different about Paulette. Her hair was simply wavy, not frizzy. She had probably used leave-in conditioner.

"You have to give the milk methodology time to work its magic," Marcus said.

Joel sipped from his soda can. "I think you need a big hat. It takes gall to walk into a classroom with a big sombrero. Any man would love you instantly."

"That is so not happening," I said.

"You want to know the only way to get a man?" Paulette asked, eyes back on the computer screen.

"What is that?" Marcus said, looking at her funny.

"The reality of the situation is that a woman must have big breasts. Why don't we tell it like it is?"

Marcus smiled but looked seriously uncomfortable, like this had been a heated conversation between them once.

127

"I've never thought I was small," I said softly.

"Oh, you're stacked," Paulette said. "Trust me." She pointed to her chest, which was way smaller than mine. She was almost a pancake on top. "But you are not displaying them goods properly. Look at that baggy clothing you're wearing."

I blushed out of shock and anger. Suddenly Paulette was the fashion expert? She was one to talk!

"If you're suggesting I go on one of those reality makeover shows, I find them disgusting."

"But oh so fascinating," Joel piped in.

"You have the goods already. We can do this for under thirty bucks. We need to go to Victoria's Secret."

Joel gulped back more of his soda and asked, "Ooh, can I go?"

"That's kind of sick," Marcus said with another big happy grin on his face.

"Who said we're doing this?" I said.

Paulette was adamant. "It's a no-brainer. How basic can you get? *Breasts high, get the guy.*"

The craziness of what she was suggesting finally struck me. "You're all going in the dressing room with me?"

"No. No one will be in that room but you. But they are, pains me to say this, men."

"I told you we were men!" Marcus said to Joel. Joel laughed.

"When you emerge from the room, they can offer valuable feedback."

"I'm not—"

"No," Paulette said adamantly. "This is a solid plan. We'll do this tomorrow. Bring a low-cut sweater or shirt so we can really give you good feedback."

The sleepy security guard opened the door. The four of us, with Paulette at the head position, filed through the glass door like a row of ducklings.

"Welcome to Victoria's Secret," a pretty Chinese customer service rep said to Paulette uneasily. Who wouldn't be startled by two middle-aged men and a woman escorting a teen into a bra store? "I'm Florence."

"We need a bra for this young lady," Paulette said confidently.

"What kind of bra?" Florence said, trying not to look worried.

"I think she needs more lift. Major va-va-voom."

The saleswoman took a calming breath. "Well, there are one or two bras that never fail—"

"Let's see them all," demanded Marcus. "Bring on the underthingies."

Paulette shot Marcus a big bad look.

Florence took another nervous glance at the two grown men tagging along for the bra purchase. "Um, what size are you?" she said to me.

"Thirty-four C," I whispered in her ear.

"Let her check, please, Jordie," Paulette said. "Your body changes when you're a teenager. The one good thing I learned from my pain-in-the-neck mother is that you should have every bra professionally fitted."

Before I could protest, out came a pink measuring tape that Florence tightly wrapped around my chest. "Well, it looks like you are a bit odd here, a thirty-five."

"Whoa!" Marcus said. "I'm in the wrong profession."

I was embarrassed beyond speech.

"I'll get the bras I have in mind," Florence said.

She came back with one white one and two black ones. All three had serious padding in them.

I grabbed the bras and took refuge in the private changing room. The situation was so humiliating that I couldn't really stay mad. I started giggling.

After I hooked on the first one, I took a hard look in the mirror. My boobs were so high, I could balance a water glass on them.

"Let's see," Paulette said impatiently outside my door.

After I put on my very low-cut taupe V-neck Gap T-shirt, I gingerly opened the door.

This time Marcus was the one who blushed. I didn't know he was capable of embarrassment. "Oh my gosh, my little innocent intern."

Joel turned to me with a silly grin on his face. "Under no circumstances are you to tell my wife what I have just seen."

"Okay," I said, taking him at face value.

Marcus and Paulette thought this was much funnier than I thought it was. Paulette even laughed again, and I was a little confused. Was I the target of a private joke they had?

"That was a joke," Joel whispered to me. "I'm as single as they come. But you do look amazing."

Paulette then said to the clerk, "We don't need to try anything else on. That's the one." To me she said proudly, "A certain Mr. Vaughan is not going to know what hit him."

"You're right. This one is a winner," Florence said to Paulette. "It directs your eyes *exactly* where they need to go," she then whispered to me.

As I got dressed, I overheard another woman getting help with a bra. "A size A is too big?" said her salesclerk incredibly loudly. "Really? It's too big? An A?"

"Yes," said a humiliated woman's voice. "Can you stop saying that?"

"Wow, I'll get you the double A."

"That's a hell of a lot of money to pay for humiliation," the angry customer said out loud to herself when the clerk had left.

How much money were these bras? I found the price tag on my bra. The "winning bra" in my hands was *way* out of my budget. I only got twenty dollars a week for my allowance, and I'd gone through my summer job savings already.

Before I could protest, Marcus grabbed the "winning" bra and took out his corporate credit card from his green Velcro camouflage wallet. "We'll put this on your account."

"What account is that?" Joel asked.

"The Boyfriend Account. She can pay us back later when she's rich and famous."

"But I charge interest," Joel warned.

"Wait," Paulette called out. "I got her a shirt in medium. Pay for this too."

"What's wrong with my shirt?"

"They call this shirt 'Jezebel' for a reason." Paulette held up a leopard skin blouse with a plunging neckline and a lace-up ruffled front.

Seriously slutty.

131

I switched into my new clothes for school that afternoon, i.e., I wore the new bra and Jezebel shirt to precalculus. When I walked into class I had my jacket zipped. Was I really going through with this cockamamy plan?

Zane saw me and shyly waved hi.

Vaughan walked in with bags under his sleepy eyes. He was yawning his head off.

"You look like hell, man," Zane said to Vaughan. It was so peculiar how for a shy guy, other guys didn't seem to intimidate him.

"Let me tell you, bro, that emergency room is *intense*."

Zane nodded. "I can imagine."

Vaughan shook his head and blew out air. "No, you *cannot* imagine. But it's kind of cool, ya know?"

Cool? I had differing thoughts about that, but I wasn't about to confess my botched attempt at lining up a companion internship with him.

Someone tapped my shoulder. Jeremy. "It's really hot in here. Why do you still have your jacket on?"

"I'm a little chilly."

"You're chilly? It's an inferno in here."

Was I ready for my big move?

I removed my jacket and draped it on my chair, trying to look as casual as possible.

Jeremy saw my "All new! Improved!" cleavage first.

"Whoa!"

Mr. Etchingham took a small breath when he saw my chest. It also seemed to me that his little bit of normal color suddenly went out of his face.

The students in my immediate vicinity made suspicious noises. Vaughan coughed. He may have been exhausted seconds before, but he suddenly looked almost perky. My advertisement definitely caught his attention. The last to sneak a look was Zane; he was predictably bright red.

The bell had yet to ring, so Jeremy took the opportunity to pass me a note.

We were very big on notes to each other, and sometimes they went back and forth three times in a minute. *That's some bra you have on.*

What bra? I scrawled back.

Your boobs are Popkin' out to the moon. What do you mean, what bra? What's with that?

I've worn this bra before.

No, you have not. Every guy in the room is looking at you.

Really?

Really.

Is Vaughan?

Vaughan? You too? Is that what this looking like a bimbette is all about?

Well, is he?

Yeah. Jeez. I didn't think you were part of his fan base.

Etchingham checked class attendance in his Delaney card seating plan book. Green cardboard Delaney cards are some leftover bit of New York public school protocol that always made me feel like we were pupils carting lunch pails in the Great Depression. For each teacher, students filled out their last name and first name and homeroom. The teacher placed the cards in rows in a Delaney book, creating a permanent seating plan for the year. At Clarkson, I never once filled out such an impersonal bit of paper. Everyone just knew who you were after a day or two.

Etchingham glanced from his Delaney book to my row and still seemed to avoid at all costs looking directly at me.

"Okay, let's have those slope homeworks. Ms. Popkin, you may want to put a jacket on."

The class collectively gasped, and someone—I'm pretty sure it was Vaughan—laughed out loud.

We passed them up.

* * *

When the end-of-class bell rang, I pretended to search for something in my messenger bag; I wanted everyone to leave before me. I took so long looking for my "something" that Zane was the only person outside in the hallway when I emerged. He was retying his retro Air Jordans.

He stood up just as I came out. He turned toward me, obviously pitying me. "So, how is your internship going?" His voice was reassuringly friendly, which, considering his shyness, was a remarkable feat. I knew he was letting me know in his own awkward way that he felt bad for my fashion error. But he made damn certain he was looking at my eyes, not my boobs.

"It's good, it's good. But I'm, uh, we're running late for French."

I put my black jacket on and zipped it up as high as the zipper would go.

Zane and I had to make a break for French if we were going to be there before the bell. I didn't walk with him, though, and he looked a bit offended that I was obviously waiting for him to go ahead. Why couldn't he just accept that Chesty didn't want to talk to anyone more than she had to? Eventually, he got the message, and he didn't look at me when I arrived in the class. Thankfully, no one else in my French class was also in my precalculus class. And this time, I was not taking my jacket off—I didn't care if I was sweating like a road worker.

On the subway ride home, I seethed again at what I had been through. And I was mad all over again at my mentors for my disgrace. The other faces on the train blurred. My face was hot and red. But I had a really big afterthought. Vaughan might be truly handsome, but Zane was so nice to me, and I had just rushed away from him. I was going to make a point of thanking him for his kindness. I changed before my mother saw me.

That night, sleep, for obvious reasons, was not happening.

11. Know Your Competition

Don't be too focused on your own account.
Never forget that there is always competition.
Check out what is happening around you.

"So, so?" Paulette said when I walked into my internship office the next morning. She was about to make a phone call and was standing, a rare position for her. It was hard not to notice her black pantsuit, which really flattered her surprisingly shapely thin body. "How did our bra girl do?"

"It went well, at first." I had hoped to keep my voice level.

"What do you mean, at first?" Marcus said suspiciously. "Whatever happened second must have been pretty rough. No offense, but you look like hell."

"That's a nice thing to say," Paulette said sternly.

"I had a really rough day yesterday, Marcus, okay? I *may* have been crying a little."

Marcus stopped in his tracks and came and sat down next to me. He removed his (surprisingly) furry coat and laid it over the back of Paulette's chair. Despite my sour mood I was highly amused by the crazy garment he was wearing; I wanted to e-mail my sister—we've had a years-running joke about men in fur coats. Someone ought to send them all a telegram: *No. It doesn't work.*

"Okay, what happened?" Marcus said sympathetically.

"What happened," I repeated, "was that my teacher said I should put a jacket on in front of the whole class—and Vaughan laughed. I feel so humiliated."

"He laughed?" Marcus said. "Maybe he was titillated."

"Time for the sombrero strategy," Joel said.

I glared at him.

"Shut up, please," Paulette said to both of them. Then she said to me, "I'm sorry that happened. We didn't want you to be humiliated—"

"Blin, anyone?" Joel asked.

"What?" Marcus asked.

"I made blini for all. My grandmother's secret recipe from Odessa. She was going to give it to a granddaughter, but I was the only one interested in her cooking. She also gave me the recipes for her famous fruit buns and an eggless mayonnaise she perfected during the war when eggs were in short supply—"

Paulette looked incredulously at Joel. "Can't you see Jordie is hurting?"

"That's why I offered her a blin."

"You don't work with lead-based paint," Marcus said very loudly. "So why are you so stupid?"

"Excuse me?" I said.

"I'm talking to Joel—why isn't the message here getting through? Shut up!"

Joel did.

I sighed. "If it suits you, I'll just learn about premiums, thank you. I don't think I'm going to be sharpening my creativity skills on the guy I have a crush on anymore."

"Why do you have a crush on him if he's the kind of guy who would laugh at you?" Paulette said. Her question was a good one.

"Look, why do you want Marcus so much even when you hate him?" I then asked.

A shocked noise came out of Paulette's mouth.

"I'm sorry, I really didn't mean to say that."

"Is this news true, Paulette?" Marcus said. "Are you secretly in love with me?"

"Not so secretly," Joel said.

"I sometimes still find you cute, that's all I'll give you," Paulette answered in a low voice.

"Cute!" Marcus squealed. "That's a lot. I'll take cute." 141
He winked at me just like Nurse Louise back in the emergency room.

I ignored the wink. I was really worried that I had offended Paulette. I hate when I talk without thinking. "Please don't have it out because of my big mouth."

Instead of answering, Paulette said, "Marcus, if you are going to have any kind of chance with me, you are going to first have to take your coat off my chair. I don't like seal fur shedding on my chair."

Marcus picked up his coat and looked at the back of the seat. There was no questioning whose chair it was: Paulette had written her name in sparkly blue nail polish on the molded yellow plastic. "It's not seal," he said. "It's imitation seal."

After that lunacy-as-usual comment I thought that maybe I hadn't actually ruined my internship by being so thoughtless, and that just maybe it was safe to smile again.

"As far as the guy goes, we've all been there, honey. I'll tell you why you like him, and I don't even have to see him. He's perfection, right?" Paulette said.

"Perfection?"

"You can't explain it, but you feel it, right? Some men have pheromones that drive me crazy—they have testosterone coming out of every pore. We don't know why we love them, but we do."

Marcus smiled in my direction and moved his eyebrows up and down like Groucho Marx.

Paulette shook her head at the sight of that, clearly annoyed with herself for revealing so much.

"Let's not make this young girl any more uncomfortable than she is," suggested Joel. "Let her learn about premiums."

"I actually had an idea about one," I said almost meekly. If I was ever going to risk relaying my mascot brainstorm, this was the moment. Things couldn't get much more Jordie Popkin–focused. Plus I had pity on my side.

They all snuck glances at each other—they were apparently highly entertained by my announcement.

Joel rolled up a chair in front of me. "So, who told you that Fred didn't like our idea?"

"No one," I said. "Oh, I'm sorry, guys. After all of your hard work—"

"Not to worry. We have another week to come up with something."

"A week?"

"That's a lot of time for us. So let's get to your idea, already."

"The season is eighteen months away," I started nervously.

"Yes, it is." Marcus's response was clipped, and I wasn't sure if he was being sarcastic.

"So are the Winter Olympics," I continued.

"And?" Paulette said.

"Do you know about the Turin mascot they unveiled this week?"

"No," Joel said.

"I do," Paulette said. "Watched all about it on *Entertainment Daily* when I raced home for that missing file—"

"So, what was it?" Marcus asked.

Paulette answered for me. "There are two of them. A boy and a girl. A block of ice and a ball of snow."

I nervously paused, then continued like a saleswoman, "Imagine having them do Winter Olympic activities. Put them on skies. Burger Man is in every country. You could have the Olympic symbols on them. They are obviously going after the youth market by designing that sort of mascot. They're already building the youth base for their own brand."

"I can't picture them." Joel went to the Internet and did an image search on Google. He called Marcus and Paulette over to the screen.

"Cute characters," Paulette said.

Marcus wasn't long in answering. "The Olympics would never stoop to that level. They are so protective of their

trademark. They would never call themselves a brand, except for their own goods—"

"But they are," I insisted.

"You," Joel said, "are a lightning-fast learner."

"She is," Paulette agreed, nodding her head toward Joel.
"They do have the official this, the official that of everything. They're not so precious. They need to make money in
consumerville."

"You *like* this idea?" Marcus asked Paulette. He had a
rather amused look on his face.

"I do, and not just because I'm trying to win our smart
little friend back."

Hearing that praise from her was a simple shot in the
arm that did wonders for me.

I glanced over toward Paulette. "Really?"

She smiled very warmly. "I think you've struck gold."

Marcus took a long hard look at Paulette and decided
she was not kidding. "Then let's do some sketches right
now."

"How about her first idea, the snow creatures on skies?"

Joel did the sketch. "What other Winter Olympics
games are there?" he asked.

"Bobsled," I said happily.

"Ice-skating," Marcus said.

Paulette rapped her marker against the whiteboard for
our renewed attention. "Others?"

After that I only half remember who said what.

"Ice hockey."

"Ski jumping."

"Luge."

"Isn't that the same as bobsled?"

"I think the sled is shorter, or something like that. There's another sliding sport, what's it called?"

"Skeleton. Those guys are insane. I watched that during Salt Lake City. No steering mechanism."

"Don't forget dogsled," Marcus said.

"Dogsledding is in the Olympics?" Joel said.

"I'm not sure about that," Paulette said.

"I think it's a demonstration sport." I surprised myself that I even knew that. "What about speed skating?"

"Ooh, that's the creepiest one. They wear those hoods, they look like condoms. Can we say that word in front of you?"

That one was definitely a Joel comment because I re-member telling him I'd have to report him to the racy-word police.

I simply couldn't believe it. The creatives were taking my idea ultraseriously.

Over the next few hours, we narrowed the list of pos-sible premiums to a figure skater, a bobsledder, a skiier, a hockey player, and a speed skater.

Instead of people's faces, the premiums would have the cute cartoony faces of Neve, the snowball, and Gliz, the block of ice.

"Joel, let's get those ideas sketched out," Marcus said when we had a consensus.

As everyone worked hard, a hot, bright sun filtered through that penthouse skylight over our department's desks.

This was a rare stretch of silence at Out of the Box. I finally understood the real reason for Joel's employment. I'd never questioned that Marcus was the team leader. And because when I first met Paulette she had been scratching that bird on her scratchboard, I'd thought she was the main artist of the trio. But maybe she was just doing that to relax. Now I knew she was all about words and wording—she was the only one with a word processing program always up on her screen. It was Joel who had now revealed himself to be the visual pro, and apparently he preferred to "sketch" with a paintbrush he took out of a paint box crusted over with countless cakes of color on top. "I'm still a bit old school," he said when he caught me looking at him a little strangely.

He amazed me by how fast he re-created those mascots in the various sports poses.

But the way they interacted as a team was what was most interesting. Their give-and-take bordered on insane. They yelled at each other often, offering better ideas and making corrections, but they never were really saying anything too mean.

"Make his arms thicker, Joel," Paulette demanded. "Olympians have really meaty hands."

"He's a bobsledder, Paulie, not a weight lifter."

Marcus occasionally neighed like a horse.

Joel speed-dried his little paintings with three long sprays from an aerosol can. After he opened up his Pagemaker program, he scanned each one onto his computer.

He printed out his artwork from his computer and then

cut and pasted them onto a white storyboard, and hand-lettered on top: OLYMPIC MASCOT PREMIUM.

The extra steps made it look impressive, really artistic.

"I think that really packs a visual wallop," Paulette said out loud, confirming my untrained thoughts.

"Okay," Joel said happily, "who is calling Daisy at Burger Man and saying we want to hit her humorless boss with another idea?"

"Who do you think?" said Marcus.

Was Paulette unnerved by his instant readiness to speak with Daisy? I was pretty sure that was the case.

"Don't we have to call the Olympics first and see about clearance?" I asked.

"Nah," Marcus said. "A lot of this industry is smoke and mirrors. If I tell Burger Man in the right way why this is a great idea, they'll come on board. Then we turn to them, one of the most powerful companies in the world, to use their muscle to convince the Olympics committee. They probably already have an advertising relationship. Just nobody probably thought to exploit the premium potential before."

"Not till you," Paulette said to me with such warmth that I was finally confident that inside her eccentric and often gruff exterior was a really nice lady.

"Now," Joel said, "we have a stack of filing for you."

"Boy, do we have filing," Paulette said.

"It's not easy suckering the interns in," Marcus said.

My grin must have taken such a dramatic turn downward that Marcus added, "We really do love your idea, and we are going to submit it. But internships come with highs and lows."

"Okay," I said to the three of them.

With their new respect for me, I really thought that was the end of the Vaughan campaign.

I was practically being treated like a peer.

12. Don't Get Smug (Yet)

Don't boast or get smug before you are
actually holding the winning ticket. No matter
how tempting that is—control yourself until
you're 100 percent sure you are the winner.

When I got home that night, I was determined *not* to tell my mother the good news about how my idea had gone over. Who knew if her second daughter's first "massive achievement" would ever come to pass?

As it was, she wasn't coming home for a while. Martin, her mean boss, was now insisting she work late, even though she'd been coming in a half hour early for over two years without extra compensation.

But I *had* to tell my father.

"Something happened?" he said intuitively as I sat down.

"Remember the mascot newsbreak?"

"Yes," he said with a small grin emerging.

"I had an idea to manufacture Olympic mascot premiums."

"How would that work?"

"The mascots would be in their various sports outfits,

equipped with their suitable equipment like ice skates or skis."

Dad nodded. "That's clever. Are you going to tell your supervisors?"

"That's the big news. I already did. They loved the idea and sat down with me and drew up sketches."

"And your mom thought you would learn nothing—" He stopped at what he heard his voice saying. "She really didn't say that, you know," he patently lied.

"C'mon—you know she did."

"Well . . ."

"Well, don't tell her a thing, please."

"Why not? Don't you want her to eat crow?"

"Wait and see if the Burger Man reps go for it. I really doubt it because my team has three different pitches for them."

Dad clicked off the television and bit into one of those doughnut-shaped peaches they've started selling in New York City supermarkets. "It's so cute how you just used the word 'team.' My little girl is all grown up."

"Dad, you overuse that expression."

"What expression?"

" 'My little girl is all grown up.' "

"When? When did I ever say that to you before?"

"That's what you said to me after I donated my Barbies to charity, and when I cooked that crown roast for your birthday."

"Even your mother never put those little paper crowns on my meat."

"You're just poking fun at me. I think I did something

really really big today. I was taken seriously by agency professionals."

"Listen, I'm not mocking you. I'm proud of you. And okay, if you want, I won't tell your mother about your remarkable achievement, but believe it or not, she is rooting for you to do well."

Just about then I heard the elevator open up and then my mother turning the bottom key in our door.

For the past few days, ever since I'd overheard her admit her growing tension with her boss, Martin, she had been wearing new clothing to work that looked straight out of a fashion magazine.

It occurred to me that maybe, just maybe, my mother was fighting for her job.

Further evidence: her high-heeled shoes made a lot of noise as she walked across our living room flooring. My mother has about twenty pairs of "sensible" flats, and before these shoes I'd never even seen her in heels.

She glanced at Dad and me so obviously engrossed in conversation on the couch. "You two have been rather tight lately." Her voice was a bit shaky.

As she slipped off her shoes and sat next to us, I took a long hard look at her.

She seemed almost strange in her new style of dress.

13. Timing Counts

When the campaign is working,
the pace can get hectic,
but don't slack off.

The subway was running late, and wouldn't you know it, I was the last one to arrive in precalculus.

Etchingham managed to give me a really nasty look even though I was sure I had not heard the new-period bell ring yet.

I saw Jeremy looking at me strangely first, but then I was aware of many other anxious eyes in the room.

Something big was up. I knew I wasn't the focus of attention this time. In my dad's old sweatshirt, I was about as sexy as a bag of potatoes.

"As I just announced to the class, Miss Popkin, with a few exceptions I was unimpressed with the class's slope homework. To think that this is a math school." He looked around the room. At Edward Carney's face, he said, "Such a look! I'm not talking about you, Mr. Carney. Relax."

The admonition for the rest of us kept going and going. The bell rang to start the new period.

"Folks, as I was saying, I am saddened by your flippant disregard for your duties. So much for the crème de la crème. What was handed in was downright pathetic. I'm talking homework, folks. You can look up the answers!" He looked back to me and said, "So, Miss Popkin, you see, I have no choice but to administer a pop quiz. As you can see before you, the mood here is rather solemn."

A quiz? I was still a bit fuzzy about the formulas we'd learned, but that never seems to change as far as math goes. I was as ready as I'd ever be. I quietly took my seat.

"So, how do you think you are going to fare?" he said to me as he handed back my slope homework. I didn't look at my mark in front of him. No way was I going to give him that pleasure.

"Fine," I heard myself say.

"We'll see, won't we?"

What was this, open season on Jordie? He was just cranking out those insults now for sport.

There was an awful silence in the room. "You may start," Etchingham said.

I turned over the exam that was already laid out on the wobbly desk. It was more of a test than a quiz—thirty questions! I got the first two easily again—that seemed to be my current standard—but the rest of the questions were killers.

Once, just to annoy Etchingham, I weighed the risks and purposely rocked my desk back a few times. He looked up from his *Daily News*, irritated.

But I got a paper cut on my thumb right after that, so my self-satisfaction was short-lived.

About thirty minutes into our collective misery, there was a knock on the door.

"Who is that?" Etchingham scowled. Our room had 100 percent attendance that day. He got up to answer the door, where there was a pizza deliveryman waiting with the most incredibly fake-looking red beard I'd ever seen. His mustache also looked like it came from a cheap costume shop. My suspicions were even further raised when he said, in a pathetic Italian accent, "Precalculus class?"

"Okay, whose joke is this?" Etchingham's voice boomed.

"*Signore, per favore*, who's paying for the order?"

"You must leave now, sir. I'm sorry someone put you up to this, but you are disrupting my classroom."

Everybody tried to refocus on the surprise quiz.

"No, no!" the deliveryman shouted. "This will come out of my pocket! There was an order here! Someone must pay!"

"Please leave," Etchingham said. "I don't like pranks."

At that, the deliveryman yelled in Italian, or what I imagine was Italian.

Ms. McClusky, the biology teacher across the hall, opened her door for a peek at the problem. The quick sight of her frightening face (bulging eyes, almost no eyebrows) rattled my nerves, and I immediately lost the thread of the problem I was trying so hard to solve.

Then something beautiful happened that forever redeemed Edward Carney in my eyes. Apparently, all that noise was also not so good for a student striving for valedictorian status.

"Mr. Etchingham," Edward said firmly, "this test was designed for a full class period, and I don't think it is right to judge us on this. I need full concentration."

"I second that," said Sara Schwartz two seats in front of him. I was shocked. Sara was in my homeroom. Even so, I didn't know her well. She had long and pretty light brown hair and warm brown eyes, but she was the mousiest person you could ever meet. Even by junior year, she had few friends. I'd long suspected that there was really a sweet person underneath all that awkwardness, like Zane, but when I'd tried to engage her in conversation, she'd barely said anything other than "Uh-huh."

With Edward and Sara's lead, our beleaguered class braved the revolution.

"Let's have it tomorrow," someone said loudly.

"Throw this one out," Jeremy said.

"This test is void, as far as I'm concerned," Zane said.

"So who is going to take responsibility for this prank, Zane?" Etchingham said.

The pizza man listened intently to the conversation, like he was listening for names.

"Who is on the order?" Zane was now crimson red.

"A Vaughan?" the deliveryman said, looking at the bill.

"Mr. Etchingham, I did not order this," Vaughan protested. "Someone is messing with me."

Why did Zane suggest to Etchingham to check the order? Was he setting Vaughan up?

"Class is dismissed," Etchingham said. "I am getting to the bottom of this, Mr. Nussman, don't you worry. I don't think for a second that you would do this. I will find out who this man is and how he got past the guard."

But the man was gone.

Etchingham raced down the hall toward the stairs.

Most of my classmates, including Vaughan, exited as well. I looked at Jeremy and Zane.

"I'm kind of hungry," Jeremy said now that my classmates could actually look at each other again.

"Me too," Zane added.

The pizza man had left the hot pizza box just outside Etchingham's door. Didn't I know that man's silly grin from somewhere? The lingering students grabbed a slice.

It came to me: that was Marcus! Was he out of his mind?

I was still sitting there floored when I heard Jeremy whispering to Zane, "You didn't do this?"

"No!" he said.

Jeremy then narrowed his eyes and looked at me for even the slightest hint that I was the culprit.

"What?" I said. "What are you trying to insinuate?"

"Is this payback for Vaughan hinting you could never be a gifted writer?"

Zane made a face at that ugly memory. I was sure now that Zane was not Vaughan's buddy.

"Jeremy, I am dumb but I am not stupid."

Etchingham returned a minute later with Myra, one of Manhattan Science's three security guards. "I have no idea where that guy went," he said. "Someone is going to pay for this."

He then realized how many of us were eating and stared in disbelief.

Jeremy said, "We didn't want the food to go to waste, Mr. Etchingham."

Myra was clutching her record book and pointed to an open page.

"There was the president of the PTA, and Ms. Herman's brother—"

"I've met him before. Obviously not the pizza delivery-man. You're going to tell Mrs. Herman her brother is sneaking pizza in?"

"Of course not," Myra said, like the possibility was almost too preposterous to mention.

Jeremy handed Myra and Etchingham each a slice of pizza. Myra walked off, talking to herself, and Etchingham sat back down at his desk, looking a little dazed even as he fumed. He glared at the desk as he ate his slice.

I glanced up at the clock in mock horror. "See you later, fellows," I said to Zane and Jeremy. Of course, I would see Zane in a few minutes anyhow. As I raced to Moskowitz's French class I passed Dr. D in the hallway. She was walking with Marcus.

Of course I couldn't say anything to him in front of my principal except hi. I shook my head at him in subtle code.

Marcus's eyes twinkled. "Hey, sis, take a minute for an introduction. This is my brilliant intern."

"We've met before," Dr. D said. She was a little cold, per her usual lovely self, but I could see she was impressed with Marcus's choice of adjective.

"Is this your first time visiting Manhattan Science?" I asked, like he wasn't the lunatic he had just proven himself to be.

Delores Herman was stopped by a vice principal who had an urgent question for her.

"Marc, just wait a second," she said to him.

"Got his photo," Marcus whispered to me when the coast was temporarily clear.

"*Whose* photo?"

"Vaughan's. There was a spy camera in my left hand."

I looked up. Was that what this insanity was about?

"Paulette wanted me to get a picture of him."

My jaw dropped.

"Close your mouth," Marcus said quietly. "My sister is trying to figure out how security could have been breached. I'm working fast to keep that guard's job."

"How did you even know where to find Vaughan?"

163

" '*The God of Room 207*' and '*I was early for seventh-period precalculus—the class we share.*' Words ring a bell?"

Dr. D was back. "Where shall we go for dinner?" She smiled warmly at me. "I so rarely get to see my brother." Her voice was really deep for a woman's voice, but quite pleasant to hear when she was being nice to other human beings. If she ever wants another career, she could narrate culture documentaries. "This is a treat. And keep up the good work, Ms. Popkin."

"So, am I supposed to be one of your buzzing agents?" Zane asked after French class. That was a term Marcus had used and I'd put in my official and private notebooks. I'd written that maybe Jeremy could sing my praises to Vaughan.

My heart practically stopped, and I tried my best to sound like I was not dumbfounded by that comment. "Excuse me? Why would you say that?"

He read from a book. My second notebook.

"Bankability of Jordie Popkin. Cute, funny."

"Zane! What are you *doing*? That is *private* property. My property!"

"I'd thought you'd want it back. You must have dropped it while you were eating pizza."

I didn't let him finish. "That was so not right to read it through."

"I didn't know who it belonged to. So I had to read it."

Like that was likely. My name was written on the inside cover. "How much did you read?" I snarled.

"I just want you to know something. Vaughan is not a very nice guy."

"And you are?"

I stormed off.

"Jordie," I heard a voice call to me.

Zane again. Bright red.

"I'm sorry. I just don't want you to get hurt. He's so into himself—"

I didn't respond. Considering how mortified he was, you'd think I could scrape together some sympathy for him. But I couldn't. As I saw it, he was a *total* ass.

I was still mad when I heard the grinding of the subway

train pulling into the station. Miraculously, there was a free seat to recover in. I remembered my slope homework, and finally looked at it.

An 80.

An 80 is so bad?

Etchingham had made it seem like I failed!

I was angry at everything and everyone now, and when my train ground again into my home station, I tore my homework into a million bits and dropped them all into the overflowing garbage can on the platform. I almost chucked my private notebook. I was going on instinct now.

The next morning I walked into the premium division of Out of the Box just as Marcus was Scotch-taping a huge blown-up photo of Vaughan onto the flip chart. Over my official crush's photo in black marker he'd written the words OPERATION VAUGHAN.

"When did you get that printed?" I cried out.

"Don't you love our new Xerox?" Joel explained. "You did not lie. Vaughan is a very good-looking boy."

Paulette, minus her glasses—even in my anger I noticed how amazing she looked—had new words of "wisdom."

"Just by his face alone, though, I'd say the God of Room 207 is greatly enamored of himself."

"You guys are out of control!" I nearly screamed. "This must stop now. Why are you so interested in my life?"

"Did you get in trouble?" Marcus said.

"No," I admitted. "You're damn lucky Mr. Etchingham

didn't connect this to me. My friend Jeremy thought it could have been my doing, but not my teacher."

"And he never will. Even if he thinks of it, he won't find a shred of evidence. We're like the SWAT team of love. I never answered you in the hallway. That was definitely not my first visit to the school—Delores has had me come in to design a few fund-raising mailings. Because I'd been in the building quite a few times to visit my sister, I basically knew the layout. And the guards know me by now. So I walked in as me—"

Joel rapped on his table with a closed fat pink felt-tip pen. "Only the bravest can go in as themselves. James Bond and Marcus Herman—"

This tag-team aren't-we-just-so-kooky mentality was old.

"Aren't you going to ask how he got the pizza in?" Joel said like an awed Robin praising Batman.

"No," I said testily.

Marcus continued anyway. "So I came in as my sister's brother, carting a bass drum in a road case—those guards have known me for years, and I fibbed about securing an instrument for the music department from a friend of the family."

"How big is a bass drum road case?" Paulette asked.

"Big enough to hide a pizza. Then in the restroom I did the old Superman switcheroo."

"You sound like a madman," Joel said like he was actually surprised at that possibility.

I'd had enough. "Do you even know what you risked?" I said. "If my teacher *had* connected me to you, I could have gotten kicked out of school!"

"You're forgetting that Marcus is your principal's brother," Paulette said.

Marcus shook his head. "Paulette's right. She would have taken mercy. We are your guardian angels. We want you to get your man. We needed to see whom we were targeting, though. Research for the Boyfriend Account. We won't charge you extra."

I stared at them. Finally, I managed to ask, "So, how's the Burger Man presentation?"

"It's in. It's in," Joel said. "Three new ideas, including yours."

Paulette sighed. "We have nothing to do but wait."

"And play with my love life."

"Come into the kitchen," Joel said. "I have a surprise for you."

I went very unwillingly.

"Come, come," he implored when I dragged my feet in the hallway.

The kitchen smelled like chicken.

Then he demanded, "Open this up."

There was an entire prepared meal in a metal pan covered by aluminum foil.

"Tomorrow you should hand this out."

"Hand what out?"

"The chicken. In my opinion men like to be cooked for. They may say they like a career woman, but they want to be fed like a little boy. If you can give him home cooking you will win his heart."

"Joel," I started.

"Yes?"

"Am I just a joke to everyone here? I've given him milk so he can subliminally link me to his mother's breast, I've bared my own chest, and Marcus delivered a pizza to my pre-calculus class. Now you want me to give him chicken?"

"That's how any war is won, my love. Keep the attack coming. Fast and furious."

Brad poked his head in the kitchen. "What do I smell? I told the mailroom guys to call me if there was anything good to eat in here—"

"Have a wing," Joel said happily. "I made plenty."

"You cook?" Brad said, impressed.

"I do," Joel said proudly.

Marcus came bolting into the kitchen. "Come back into the room, my people."

We all looked at him a bit blankly.

"Chop-chop. Big news."

This time we complied, including Brad.

"I just got off the phone. They looked over the proposals. They are bonkers on the Olympic idea."

"What?" I practically screamed. My hatred instantly left me. All three creatives swooped upon me in congratulations. We did an impromptu game of ring-around-the-rosie without the words.

"We are so very proud of you," Marcus said. "Yes, you are our little protégée. But you've displayed genius right out of the gate. I knew you had it in you."

I blushed and lowered my eyes before all that amazing praise.

"So you love us again?" Joel said.

"Oh, goodness," Paulette said to me after a wide grin.
Marcus walked back in the room, and he sat down next
Paulette. "You, my lovely, are too much of a distraction
is week."

I swear she was about to cry.

I laughed. "I didn't say that."

"They had some serious issues, though. T[...]
hammer out a few things for them, and the [...]
tion has to get past the big boss."

Paulette reached over to the costume hat [...]
me wear a gold foil crown for the rest of my da[...]

Joel handed me a chicken leg as Marcus s[...]
decided that in order for us to give you credit[...]
let us continue to help you win over Vaughan.[...]

"This is really good. What's in the seasoni[...]
could distract them from focusing on my personal[...]

"Who's Vaughan?" Brad asked as he hurled [...]
bone into Paulette's wastebasket. Perfect shot. [...]

Paulette picked up the bone with a napkin [...]
it back to him. "Food trash in the kitchen, plea[...]
to Brad, as Joel not so discreetly shooed him aw[...]

I finally got around to saying, "You got cont[...]

"Even better," she whispered. "I finally foll[...]
that new operation I've been reading about tha[...]
eyes in one visit to the ophthalmologist. I never [...]
again."

"Let me look at your eyes," I said. They wer[...]
loveliest shade of blue. "They have a sleepy qualit[...]

"Is that a bad thing?"

This time I was determined to flatter her, no[...]
"No, like Bette Davis. My father thinks young [...]
was the sexiest actress that ever was."

She gave me a doubtful squint.

"Seriously," I assured her.

14. Don't Waste Time or Money—
Brand X: The Boyfriend Account

You've had some bumps and learning curves.
But by now you should be able to
think on your feet. If he is a known brand
you want to be associated with, then you
need to make yourself more than
just the unknown Brand X.
In other words: full speed ahead....
Remember, you don't have time
or money to waste.

They begged, what can I say? And now that the "operation" was officially named, I actually enjoyed their meddling.

There were two operations really: the half-serious one of getting Vaughan to ask me out, and the serious one of securing the Burger Man account.

I suspect my tasks as far as Vaughan was concerned were mostly dreamed up by my thirtysomething friends to entertain themselves.

"Brand identity," Joel said one day. "You have to brand yourself. You need a catchphrase."

"Maybe she could tattoo it on her arm," Brad said from his usual perch by our door.

Joel looked at me intently. "Imagine you're a better-tasting cola introduced in a nationwide rollout. . . . What's your slogan?"

I was not going to walk around school shouting a slogan. (What did he want me to say, "Pop one on Popkin"?) "Can I really act like this? My mom hates her boss because he's a 'shameless self-promoter.' "

"Does anyone still think like that anymore in the age of the Internet? For goodness' sake, everyone on Earth seems to create a Web site. Since you have neither, you are not a self-promoter."

But another item of news was to interest me even more.

At the end of French class, there was a call over the intercom for Jordan Popkin to go to Dr. D's office.

An entire roomful of eyes searched mine for any giveaway of what that scary announcement was about. Was everyone in my family okay?

I gritted my teeth as I hurtled down the hallway to the opposite side of the floor. I swallowed drily before knocking.

"Sit, sit," Dr. D said.

She looked so much like Marcus just then that for a split second I thought it was him again in a wig, pulling a new prank.

"I understand you are helping my brother tremendously," said Dr. D.

"I hope so."

"Well, I have let the paper know."

"It's good material," said a young man's voice. I hadn't even noticed Perry Nelson, the editor in chief of our school paper, in another chair against the wall. "But there is so much going on, we might not need the Olympics stuff. Overkill."

While Vaughan had a lot going for him, Manhattan Science also had Perry.

In addition to being our paper's editor, he was also in a popular local rock band with three college students. Can you imagine any college kids hanging around with a high schooler? And not only did the members of Chuckhole hang around him, but they'd also made him their lead singer.

What the hell was gorgeous Perry talking about? What was the big news?

There was a knock on the door, and in walked Mrs. Kleinman.

She had a bunch of white roses in her hand.

"Hi, champ!" she said in *my* direction.

She must have sensed the hesitation in my face. She gave me a long, appraising glance and peered over at Dr. D. "You didn't tell her."

"We were waiting for you, Adrienne."

Mrs. Kleinman gave me a smile of approval and said, jubilantly, "Jordan Popkin of Manhattan, your essay won the National Council of Teachers of English Achievement Award in Writing. First prize. In the *country*."

My eyes scanned the room in disbelief. I held back my shriek. "Really?" I said almost silently.

"Now, what was the essay on, exactly?" Perry said. I think he was proudly impassive.

"Punk rock," I sputtered. "How it was invented in America by kids who weren't at all financially deprived—"

"And how England was facing societal devastation that

made their youth anger more real to record buyers," my ex–English teacher finished for me.

I smiled at her. "You say that better than I can!"

"You did just fine!" She laughed.

The coolest kid in our high school looked at me intently with a touch of fascination. "That essay"—he paused for a second—"sounds really *cool*."

"You know, dear," said Dr. D, "I am grateful for such a positive spotlight on our school. And it's not even to do with math and science."

"As I'm always saying, kids have different skill sets," Mrs. Kleinman said.

Dr. D ignored her. "Because of your work with my brother and your knack for English, I'm reconsidering what I said to you and your friends. I think we should open up internships to match talents."

Mrs. Kleinman fanned the air in disbelief. "Sensational, Delores! I have quite a few other kids in my classes who have genuine writing talent. And they go here for their parents, but they flounder in math or science. I'd love to get some of the outstanding kids in my current essay workshop apprenticing at one of the great literary magazines in Manhattan. We have a unique opportunity to use this city's fabulous resources as a learning tool."

"Look what you started," Dr. D said to me, almost adoringly.

It was so, so, so flattering.

* * *

I was still coming to terms with the news when I emerged from the room. I was so dazed that I left my house keys in my locker.

When I got home I buzzed and buzzed. Where was my father? I sat outside on my doorstep, and about fifteen minutes later he walked out of the elevator with three stuffed plastic grocery bags.

"Forgot your keys?"

"I had good reason."

"Aliens?"

"Hurry up and open the door. This is big."

"Okay—" he said inside.

"Do you remember that essay I wrote after reading your books about punk rock bands?"

"Very much so. I was glad I had such influence over you."

"Good, because that very essay just won the National Council of Teachers of English Achievement Award in Writing, and I was called into my principal's office and the editor in chief of our school—"

Dad's face lit up. "Is there *money* involved?"

"Dad! Does money matter here? I *think* there is money coming, but I forgot to ask."

"Let's call your mother."

And we did.

When Mom came home, *she* had a huge bouquet of red roses for me.

I don't think I ever saw my mother so proud of me. All night, she called everyone she knew. Grandma Pearl first, of course.

And then my sister at Princeton.

Dad had looked up the amount on the Internet by then. "And she even earned herself five hundred dollars," he said on the other phone extension.

"Not quite a Princeton scholarship," I said.

"I wasn't comparing!" Dad cried guiltily.

Sari interrupted: "My little sister rocks!"

At school, it was almost impossible, but I kept my mouth shut about winning the big prize. I decided not to tell Jeremy or even Clara about it. In two days there was going to be a big story on me in the school paper. I really wanted the dramatic surprise of being a success. Clara had her moment with the *Times*. Would she be as jealous of me as I was about her *Times* internship? More, probably. Why did that feel kind of good?

When I got to school after my internship two days later, the first person to say anything to me was Vaughan.

"Hey, Jordie, I saw that article. So wild."

"Thanks."

"I knew it was coming, though."

"What do you mean?"

"From Perry."

I'd forgotten that Vaughan and Perry were friends.

Everyone in class apparently had seen the article too.

Even Etchingham took a few seconds to clap his hands. "Well done, Miss Popkin."

Forget about the award. *That* was probably the biggest surprise of the year.

Well, almost.

Outside class Vaughan pulled me to the side. "So, are you going to the Halloween dance with anyone?"

"No. . . ."

One of our classmates was yapping on her purple cell phone and immediately stopped to listen. So Vaughan motioned for me to follow him a few feet closer to another classroom door.

"Would you like to go with me?"

The sensation of screaming for joy in my head was new. "With you?" I said almost inaudibly.

"I know it's such a bourgeois thing, but, well, yeah, I thought it might be fun."

"I'd love to go with you," I said, my voice back.

He gave me one of his devastating grins. "I better get your phone number then, huh?"

Jeremy jerked around from the stairwell when he saw me writing something on a paper for Vaughan. I don't think he could have heard us.

He waited for me. "What was *that* about?" he asked.

I stopped the hole with a little lie. I could see why Clara liked the Big Surprise. In another questionable flash decision, I decided I would surprise my friends again with more wild news, but this time at the Halloween dance. I'd experienced being the center of attention, and it felt good.

"He wanted my e-mail. He's doing a walkathon."

"Oh." It was a pretty pathetic thing for me to say, but despite what my mother thought in those days, I didn't usually fib, and Jeremy had no reason to think I was snowing him.

Later on that day, I sat in my bed for hours thinking about reaching my goal. I think it was being taken seriously that won Vaughan over. Although I'm sure a peek at my elevated breasts didn't hurt the cause.

Around seven o'clock, I heard the phone ring. Before I could pick it up, my mother did.

"Can I tell her who is calling?" she said.

Who would be calling me on my parents' line?

"It's a gentleman named Vaughan," she said, and I sprang up so fast that I could feel her curiosity. I could have sworn I gave Vaughan my cell number. I guess I had panicked so much when he asked me to the dance that I defaulted to the number I've known longest.

Since Mom had handed me the cordless phone, I was able to move myself to my room.

"So, you're home on a Friday night too," Vaughan said.

"My mother needed me tonight," I replied.

"Yeah, well, I just didn't make any arrangements."

He was so much more confident than me for admitting the truth. In actuality I just hadn't heard of any Friday parties going.

"Do you want to catch a movie tonight? I mean, if you can get out of your obligations—"

"Did you have one in mind?"

"Do you like horror? Drama?"

"I love movies in general."

"Me too."

What I really liked was romantic comedies, but as every girl knows, that is a dumb thing to say to a guy.

"Why don't you meet me by the multiplex on Third Avenue and Eleventh Street and we'll see what we like."

"I'll give you a call back," I said. And then I gave him my cell number too.

After I called him to confirm that I could come, we agreed to meet in a Japanese teahouse called St. Alps, where he said "Japanese hipsters" hung out. He went on to say that there was a huge Japanese hipster scene in the area, and was most surprised that I had never heard of Angel's Share, a sake bar hidden above one of the stores on East Ninth Street. "You see everyone there. Sean Lennon. The Beasties."

"I don't think I can get in. I don't have a fake ID."

"How can you be a teen living in the city without a fake ID? Don't you go to nightclubs, rock concerts?"

I felt mighty inadequate as I said, "I've been to a few all-ages shows at Irving Plaza."

"We have got to get you a fake ID. My friend Ben King makes amazing fake IDs. Every time I've been carded I've gotten in."

I was really surprised by this news, because even though I knew Ben was edgy, I didn't think he would risk jail time. "But the drinking age is twenty-one and you're sixteen. How can they not tell?"

"King is a genius."

* * *

Vaughan and I never made it to the movie theater. We ordered two bubble teas with little pearls of tapioca floating in them. I ordered the almond blend and he got a mango one. It was a strange but nice-tasting beverage. I let a few tapioca balls roll on my tongue as I listened to the story of how he'd lost his official internship notebook and finally found it in his kid sister's toy box ripped to pieces—apparently Vaughan had a sister who was twelve years younger than him because his mother had remarried. "She's four and still gets off on putting things into holes and slats, but she already has a modeling contract."

It started drizzling, and then the rain bucketed down. It was easiest to sit and talk some more. I haven't had too many first dates—two to be exact—so I wasn't sure what to talk about.

He told me about a camping trip he took with the Ultimate Frisbee team, which included Perry and another senior who I had never heard of.

"You don't know Teddy? He's captain of the Ultimate Frisbee team? His father holds the ambassadorship to some European country—Belgium, I think."

Not only did I not know Teddy, but I was also sure none of my B-list friends knew about this camping trip. In some schools, the football gods reign. But at Manhattan Science, it was the academically excelling Ultimate Frisbee team members who were the exalted.

That ultrapopular clique was so mysterious to me (and

the majority of the student body) that I had no idea that Vaughan was even on the team. Didn't you have to be a cool senior to be asked? Vaughan quickly figured out that I had never been at a game, and proudly explained some of the rules to me. "Ultimate is a noncontact sport played by two seven-player teams. Come to the next match. We're playing Brooklyn Tech in Central Park next weekend."

That offer, counting today and the upcoming dance, was *three* dates.

Eventually the Halloween dance came up.

"Do you want to coordinate a costume?" he said.

"Did you have something in mind?" Did he mean to make it obvious to the school that we were together? Was this nirvana or what?

"No, you pick an idea. I really can't care less about the dance. I just wanted to hang out with you."

What followed was one of the lamest ideas I've ever had.

"I could go as Charlotte from *Charlotte's Web*," I said to Vaughan. "You could be Charlotte's spiderweb."

He stretched out the neck of his black-ribbed turtle-neck. "You want me to be a spiderweb?"

The dumbness of my suggestion hit me when he repeated it back to me. "I guess since you're a boy you never read that story—"

"Don't be so sexist. Of course I did. Everybody's read *Charlotte's Web*."

Vaughan, surprisingly, was suddenly fine with the suggestion. "I guess coming as a spiderweb is better than what my girlfriend at camp made us dress up as."

"What was that?"

"Raggedy Ann and Raggedy Andy."

I smiled.

"Katie," he confided in hushed tones, "was so not happening. But we were only fourteen at the time."

Then he moved his chair around next to mine and said, "Hey, you, come here, give me a kiss."

At just the right moment, his tongue found mine, just like in the few R-rated movies Clara and I have snuck into. I was floating on cloud nine.

"Let's get out of here," he said, and we walked out into the rain.

The night had turned gusty as well as rainy, and we gave up on forward motion. He stuck his hand out for a cab, and once we were inside asked me in front of the driver for the address of my building.

My date not only kissed me in the cab, he kissed me in the lobby for a long time.

This is the one time I was grateful that my parents could not afford a doorman building.

After a long Monday morning in which Marcus kept going in and out of our room to make private calls, he twisted his fingers around his pencil as he addressed me. "Have you eaten, my friends? How about an indoor clambake?"

"First you need a pail of clams," I said jokingly.

"Ah, come this way, my lady."

Lunch was, and I kid you not, a pail of clams. Marcus

was talking all strange around me, very fast, something about how he had bought three dozen near him at the best fish store in the city. He'd set up a Bunsen burner in the conference room. He made our team wear straw hats like we were at a beach party as he cooked the clams in a pan coated with melted butter.

I could tell from Paulette's face that she was suspicious as well. "Get your bad news out as quickly as possible," Paulette said suddenly to Marcus.

What bad news was this? Involving whom?

Marcus coughed once, pulled the hat down over his eyes, and said softly, "Your Olympic mascot idea didn't get the go."

"What? You lost the account?" Was this my fault? I didn't mean to cause ruin for them.

"No, no, calm down," Marcus said. "They are going with our third idea."

"For *The Eggcups?*"

"Yes, indeed. The head of Burger Man wants a safer bet. Safer means a Disney movie. No one in the industry has vision anymore."

"Wow" was all I could say.

"Except us," he added nervously. "And that means you too."

Then they all looked at me like they would desperately need to coax happiness back into my life.

"Are you okay?"

"Yes, of course. It was amazing they even considered it. . . ."

Paulette clucked her tongue. "You're such a mature young lady. Such composure."

"Well, I've had other good news since I've seen you last."

"Which is?" Paulette asked.

"I actually won a national high school essay contest."

"Oh, sensational!" Paulette exclaimed.

"Which one?" Marcus asked.

"You know specific high school essay contests?" Joel asked drily.

"A few," he said.

"The National Council of Teachers of English Achievement Award in Writing."

"I was hoping you wouldn't say that," Marcus said, even as he slapped me on the shoulder to congratulate me. "I submitted an essay for that. There were a hundred finalists, and I didn't even get on that list." He looked at me. "You did say you were a finalist, didn't you? My teacher said the chances of winning were infinitesimal."

"You're not a good listener, are you?" Paulette said to Marcus.

"Um, I won," I confirmed sheepishly.

Marcus had a funny expression on his face for a second, and then he dropped to the ground. "Oh, Your Highness! I'm not worthy!"

I grinned and then said in an affected royal voice, "I'm sorry you didn't win. What was your essay about?"

"Barbecues," Marcus said with a straight face.

"Barbecues?" Paulette, Joel, and I asked in unison.

"I still remember my opening line: 'An expert barbecuer knows how to tenderize anything.' "

Everyone chuckled, but there was another faint sound of laughter coming from behind us.

Brad was listening in again.

"Help yourself to some clams," Marcus said.

"I will," Brad said.

"Go ahead and laugh, my friends," Marcus said, "but my English teacher liked it. I'll tell you what won my year, some stupid shallow essay about the fall of the shah of Iran."

"Barbecuing being a much better essay topic," Paulette said.

"I know. I was hurt. I'm sure that's why my sister didn't tell me that my intern took the gold. She was shielding my fragile soul."

Paulette patted him on his bare knee. (It was forty degrees outside, but he was wearing beach shorts.)

Joel rolled his eyes at Brad and then turned back to me. "Is there money involved?"

I looked at him. "That's what my dad asked me. I asked him, and I'll ask you—is *that* what counts?"

"College costs money."

"A token amount. A few hundred dollars."

"Stop picking on the wunderkind," Marcus said.

I smiled big and removed my straw hat. "But there's more," I said dramatically as I laid it down on the table.

"Where do you go from there?"

"He asked me to the Halloween dance."

"Who?" Marcus said.

"Who do you think?" I said with a theatrical toss of my head.

"No!" Paulette yelled.

"Am I missing something?" Marcus asked.

"And you're our creative chief?" Joel laughed.

"Operation Vaughan was a success."

Marcus let out a doglike yelp. "That too!"

Paulette kissed me on my head. "Sweetie, I am so happy for you. Tell us everything. Eggcups bore us, as you know."

And I did, about the article in the paper, the dance, the surprise extra date. They were oohing and aahing at every detail.

"Did you kiss?" Joel said.

"Yes," I said.

"What was it like?"

"*That* I'm not telling."

Joel looked knowingly at Brad again, whose small face was much too orangey from the tanning salon he frequented across the street. "I so want to be back in high school," Brad pined.

Spending sixth period in precalculus as "Vaughan's girl" was truly a weird, wonderful experience.

Vaughan winked at me once. That's all. I took his cue to be chill about things and didn't gaze over at him.

"We'll speak tonight," he whispered softly at the end of class.

As if that was not enough attention for the week, after French when I opened my padlock to get out my coat, I knelt by my locker to tie my sneaker. When I stood up, Zane was standing next to me.

"Are you going to the Halloween dance?" he said.

I gave him a forced smile and surprisingly he gave me a huge smile back.

"I know you despise me, but—"

Yes, he was so shy. Yes, he was stupid enough to read my personal notebook. But he was really rather cute. But I had Vaughan to walk in with. *I have no regrets*, I said to myself, remembering the Edith Piaf song from French. I just couldn't get myself too worked up over what might have been with a B-lister like myself.

I remembered Paulette's words from a few hours prior. "Give your bad news as quickly as possible."

"I'm really sorry, Zane, but I'm already going with someone else."

His response, "Oh," was only half spoken. "Did you get back together with Jeremy?"

Now, how did Zane find out I had ever dated Jeremy? I was surprised that he knew this historical detail. My three-day relationship with Jeremy was still not widely known among my classmates. We'd never held hands in school. We'd done all of our kissing at each other's houses. So it was evident that Zane had actually discussed me with someone I knew well, maybe even Jeremy himself.

"I'm going with Vaughan," I said as nicely as possible, but there was definitely a little extra pride in my voice.

The light from the hallway ceiling glared directly into my eyes as I waited for his response. There was no comment for a long pause, so I assumed he wasn't taking this too well.

I shifted a few inches away and I could see he was as red as a beet.

"With Vaughan?" he said. "Really?"

"Really."

"So your plan worked." He didn't sound too happy about that.

"You could say that," I said, a bit meanly. He wasn't helping his cause.

"Wow. Since when have you been a couple?"

"It's new. Since Friday."

I shrugged. With the English prize still fresh in my mind, and the developments with Vaughan, I was very big on myself that afternoon. "He never read my notebook," I joked. I emphasize, it was a *joke*. But it went down like jellied veal at a kid's birthday party.

"Yeah. Have fun," was all he could say as he made a quick dash to the exit. I wanted to call out that I was only teasing, but now I could tell by Zane's weird gait that he was fuming.

He was moving so fast that he was almost running.

During our evening phone call, I stupidly told Vaughan that Zane had asked me to the dance after him. Vaughan wanted me to replay the moment in great detail.

"Did he seem cocky?"

"No, he was very sweet about it."

"What did you feel?"

I left out all the details about my notebook, of course. "He's so passive. I was so shocked that he'd worked up his courage. I hope he can take someone nice. He's really starting to break out of his shell these days."

"Hey, where do you get your name from?" Vaughan unexpectedly asked Zane the next afternoon in precalculus.

Zane looked at him uneasily, and so did I. What the *hell* was Vaughan doing?

"My dad is a big Zane Grey fan."

"Who?" Vaughan asked. There was something so fake about the way he said that, like he knew damn well who Zane Grey was.

"My parents told me that he was a writer who pioneered the Western adventure genre back in the twenties. Did you ever hear of *Riders of the Purple Sage?*"

"Well, that's incongruous."

"How's that?"

"Well, since you're so passive—"

Zane's eyes flashed in anger. "Excuse me?"

That comment was just so off. "Vaughan, that's . . ." I was so shocked, I couldn't even get any words out.

My new boyfriend looked at my open stare and snapped, "You're the one who said Zane was passive. That you felt kind of sorry for him."

"I have to go," Zane said. "Go" sounded like "g-g-g-o." If Zane was any redder, he'd pass out.

"I can't believe you," I spat at Vaughan, but Zane sprinted out of the room so fast, I don't think he could have heard me say that.

"Why are you looking at me shaking your head?" Vaughan asked.

Our new twosome just stood there fighting. It took a very long time to calm me down, but eventually Vaughan made me agree to meet him at the coffee shop down the block.

"I was just kidding," he said, and then kissed my cheek.

I was still fuming as I opened the glass doors of the coffee shop after school had ended.

We sat at the only two counter seats that were available. There was spilled sugar and splotches of purple jam all over our section. Vaughan caught the eye of a waiter behind the counter, and then he apologized profusely after our table was cleaned. I remember three important words he said to me, that I was:

Cute.

Funny.

Sexy.

Sexy! This conversation was changing my sense of where I stood in the world, and it took all my willpower not to do a full-circle swivel in delight. I never thought anyone so desired by the entire school would or could feel that way about me.

With that level of sweet talk, I forgave him.

As Vaughan sprinkled vinegar onto my fries like he said

they do in England—he'd been there once for a whole summer—he promised he'd apologize to Zane and say he had added words to our conversation.

We kissed again.

"Zane who?" I said out loud, and Vaughan grinned.

A minute later we were happily planning our costumes.

15. When Congratulations Are in Order, Don't Blow It

You landed the account. But only pat
yourself on the back for a minute.
Now reevaluate—and as always, remember
to focus. As they say in the business:
Did you underprice? Overprice? Time for
needed adjustments based on both
what the account wants from you—
and what you want for the account.
You not only want to get the account,
you want to keep it.

That Saturday, Vaughan came to my house four hours early so we could pull together our getups. I had begged my parents to go to a museum or a movie. Earlier in the morning my father poked his head in my room and announced, "I hope you don't mind, sweetheart, but your mother and I have decided we'd much rather see you squirm." Even though he was razzing me, I shot him an evil look. I still don't know where they went, but the end result was that they were not in the apartment anymore. Vaughan and I were alone.

"Can I get you anything to drink?" I asked him after a quick kiss hello.

"You don't possibly have orange juice?"

"I do."

I poured him a glass. "How's your little sister doing? Still slotting?"

He snorted a little bit, but before answering he quickly checked out the living room CD rack—hopefully the Popkin selection didn't offend his sensibilities too much. "My sister is driving my parents crazy. They put her to sleep in her own bed but she sneaks between them in the middle of the night. Every time they wake up, she's right in the middle."

"It would probably be very calming to do that. Doesn't part of you want to do that a bit?"

"Sleep between my parents?"

"Yeah."

"No. That's kind of disgusting."

"Just on a really bad day. They'd be wearing pajamas."

"You forget, right now I live with my stepdad, not my real dad. To sleep with my parents would mean getting divorced parents in the same bed. They despise each other. The thought of sleeping between those two now is about as appealing as sleeping between scaly monsters."

I smiled.

"So, you got the yarn, right?" We had decided to use white yarn as Charlotte's spider thread.

I pointed to a shopping bag. "Right here."

"Didn't her web say things?"

"Yeah," I said to the God of Room 207 now seated on my couch drinking juice. "Templeton the rat brought her bits of garbage and she copied advertising words off of them."

"Like what?"

"*TERRIFIC!*"

"Anything else?"

"*RADIANT!*"

"I'm sure there was something funnier."

"Well, I think I know what you mean, but you're not going to walk into a dance with the words SOME PIG on your sweatshirt."

He smirked. "That would be so funny. That's exactly what we have to write."

I borrowed my dad's bottle of glue from his home office supply drawer. Vaughan painted the words SOME PIG on with glue, as well as a decent web design. We laid the yarn on. The strands dried pretty quickly, and then he pulled the black sweatshirt over his head.

Once we'd draped sufficient extra white yarn all over the rest of him, careful not to block the all-important wording, we started in on my spider costume. I needed eight legs, and Vaughan had the brilliant suggestion of using three pairs of my black tights and pushing long cardboard tubes from cheap bulk wrapping paper into them.

199

My mother is just the kind of consumer who never bothers with inspired presentations and buys just that kind of wrapping paper in bulk. I attacked her closet and produced exactly six long rolls that Vaughan slipped the cardboard innards out of.

Vaughan had me turn around after I fit myself with the costume. "Something's missing."

I looked in my mirror. "I know."

"Think arachnid," he said.

We looked at a picture of a spider online and saw that the abdomen is the thing that sticks off the back. Vaughan said that I needed more bulk in the back to get that effect.

"I'll give it a try," I decided out loud.

I shoved a small couch pillow in the back of my own black sweatshirt. With both agreed that I now looked very spiderlike.

The dance coordinators had rented a strobe light and a smoke machine, so it took a little while to make out what everybody was wearing, and who was with whom.

Vaughan held my hand as we made our way to the back of the room. Since he mostly hung out with seniors, I'm sure he felt awkward, but not as awkward as I did.

He reached for my hand to walk farther into the room, but accidentally reached for one of the fake spider limbs. His smile after his mistake was so infectious that I thought, *We're going to have a blast. Stop being so nervous.*

There was a massive backdrop of ghosts and witches and pumpkins ahead of us.

"Who volunteers for this crap?" Vaughan asked. I was silently angry, as I knew that Willie was one of the artists who did the work. I've always found knee-jerk cynicism so boring.

Edward Carney had a big letter O framing his face, and I thought he was possibly dressed like an icicle.

"What the hell is he?" Vaughan whispered to me.

"A cold letter O?" I guessed.

Vaughan took it upon himself to ask him.

Before answering, I saw Edward look at my hand interlocked with Vaughan's. As he widened his eyes he said, "I'm absolute zero."

"Okay," Vaughan said. "Explain."

"Absolute zero is the temperature so cold that nothing can move. It's the coldest temperature there is."

"Clever," Vaughan said, and Edward smiled appreciatively.

When he was out of sight, Vaughan said, "Jerk."

We moved on. I couldn't see any of my friends yet. Eventually Vaughan spotted Ben King, his fake ID connection, who was dressed as a vodka bottle that read ABSOLUT STONER.

Vaughan whispered that Ben's homeroom teacher was continually trying to nail Ben, but he could never kick him out of school, because he rarely smoked weed on school property and had never been caught. "And furthermore, he is Carney's fiercest competition for valedictorian status."

"Get out of here! What's his grade point average?"

"Four-point-oh."

I was astonished. "Ben King? So you think that Dr. D wants to keep him around just in case he gets an Intel award?"

He nodded. "You know as well as anyone how she loves good press on her students."

Tara from Alabama was wearing a mask of big red lips. I didn't know too much about modern art junior year, but I did grow up in a city with great museums, so you pick things up. I correctly guessed she was referencing that famous painting of an enormous pair of lips. (Later on in the year I learned that an artist named Man Ray had painted it in the thirties.) I bet most of the guys never understood her costume, but the rest of her body was so perfectly packaged in a revealing black dress and slingbacks that even the adult punch servers kept sneaking looks. Who was her date? Perry, the editor/singer. So much for my coup—Tara had been asked by a senior, the most desirable senior, to come to a junior dance!

Vaughan and Perry high-fived, and Perry greeted me warmly. Tara looked surprised to see me at Vaughan's side but said hi to me just as warmly.

Was I now part of the "it" crowd? Was that what was going on here? Our cluster of people included four members of the ultimate Frisbee team coordinated as the quintessential seventies band, Kiss. You could tell they were fine-looking even under all that makeup, and you could also tell who their dates were—the ones with white greasepaint on their lips or cheeks from wherever they had been kissed.

Ben King and Vaughan went to the men's room for a second, and I was left chatting with Ben's date, a pretty blond girl from another high school with no costume on, and also one of the Kiss impersonators. I saw Jeremy out of the corner of my eye. I half wanted to shield him from Tara and Perry, but he was grinning from ear to ear. He was with Blanca, a hookup that was *his* big surprise.

Blanca was dressed as a ham. Have you ever read *To Kill a Mockingbird*, by Harper Lee? Even if your school doesn't make it a requirement, trust me, it's really good. It's one of those books that make you laugh and also get you livid about the world's wrongs, and inspire you to eventually do something about them. I loved it so much that I had asked my father to rent the movie from Netflix. There's a terrifying scene when the narrator, a white girl named Scout, who, while dressed as a ham, is attacked by the main villain in the book, the very racist Mr. Ewell. Atticus Finch is Scout's courageous father, a lawyer trying to prove a black man had not raped Ewell's daughter, but merely talked to her. When the slightly dim but kind town outcast, Boo Radley, saves Scout from the attack, she gratefully runs to Atticus in that ham outfit she'd been walking home in from a Halloween party. I think Lee's insertion of a bit of humor in the situation made the scene completely readable and even more compelling.

Everybody in my junior class had to read *To Kill a Mockingbird* our sophomore year, so most people got it right away.

"How come you're not Atticus?" a hairy guy named Kevin dressed as Marilyn Monroe said to Jeremy.

True to form, Jeremy came dressed as the nerdy New York film director Woody Allen at a New York Knicks basketball game. Woody Allen is the Knicks' number one celebrity fan and gets about ten close-ups on TV every game. In addition to wearing a team jersey, Jeremy had tousled his hair and worn horn-rimmed glasses and loose brown cord pants. The freaky thing was that he looked just like a young Woody Allen. It was inspired.

I was admiring the raging genius of both of my friends' costumes when Vaughan came back and slipped an arm around my waist. Both Jeremy and Blanca gasped.

I was sure Vaughan smelled like pot, but I didn't say anything. I'm not from Planet Prissy, but for the most part I was just as much silently antidrug back then as I am now.

That night, though, I imagined I was going to have to

smoke a good deal of pot over the next year to stay on the A-list, and this is so weird: I quickly came to terms with that.

This is also going to sound incredibly shallow, but suddenly I couldn't wait to see whom Clara would bring. Or not bring. We'd not really discussed the dance, which was unusual for us. She'd suggested we go together, and I'd fibbed and made an excuse, saying I'd see her there.

Well, she came alone. I think she was supposed to be a sixties love child. Her costume consisted of a vintage white top with lace edges and denim landlubber bell-bottoms. But to tell you the truth, that's how she pretty much dressed every day.

"Who did you come with?" she asked Vaughan.

"Jordie." He squeezed my hand.

She looked at me and I nodded. Because of her ambushed facial expression I was instantly sorry I had kept this from her. Meanwhile, Vaughan thought back to where he'd met her. "Were you in my English class?"

"Yes," she said, still with a bit of hostility toward me on her face.

"You were an amazingly good writer."

Clara looked at him, and he smiled ever so charmingly.

I interjected, "She still is. Clara got the *New York Times* internship."

"At the science section?" Vaughan said.

Clara nodded. "It's my good luck."

"I'm sure luck has nothing to do with it. What sorts of things have you been working on?"

"I've mostly been helping the editors with the research.

There's a big piece on platypuses I was helping them out with this week."

"What's new in the world of platypuses?" I cracked, trying to regain the steering wheel.

Clara answered Vaughan instead of me. "Did you know that the platypus has ten sex chromosomes? But the best thing is that they're allowing me to do my very own piece, an insider's view of Manhattan Science internships."

"Really?" I said, mostly delighted for her, even though she was doing that answering-Vaughan thing. I couldn't be too selfish, having so recently won that essay contest. "In print?"

"In print," she confirmed to Vaughan.

"Really, Clara?" She had not breathed one word of this to me. But this time I playfully called her on it. "So, how come I haven't heard this?" *And PS, how can you be mad at me when you're doing your own Miss Mysterious act?*

Her voice toward me had an unexpected sharp tone. "Well, honestly, it's a bit awkward. Of course I want to feature my best friends, but I know that your internship would not be appropriate for the science section. It's going to be a political nightmare to figure out which of the students to profile. Jeremy's internship is just not interesting enough and—"

Luckily, Jeremy and Blanca were now dancing.

"C'mon, get over the guilt. Jeremy and I wouldn't expect you to profile us. How about Vaughan? Vaughan's in the emergency room."

"That could work."

Vaughan smiled appreciatively at me. "What's wrong with Jordie's internship?"

"Well, you know who she's working for, don't you?"

A sudden thought crossed Vaughan's mind. "You know, I never really asked you, but where *is* your internship?"

I hesitated for a second and then said, "At a company called Out of the Box."

"It's fascinating what they do there, of course," Clara said, primping her hair as she spoke.

I looked at her intently. It was just something about her tone of voice again.

"Which is?" Vaughan asked.

"They make premiums," I said quickly. "The spot freakishly got through Dr. D's vetting, and Becky thought it was a good match for me, so I'm the only one she—"

"Premiums?" he repeated. "What are premiums?"

"Advertising giveaways. Toys for kids' meals."

"Why would you accept *that?*"

"Excuse me?"

Vaughan, even as my date, couldn't help a sneer. "Don't you feel like crap at the end of the day? It's not only not brain surgery, it's consumerism at its worst."

I felt sick at his words.

"I like my experience. It's really eye-opening. I mean, they're fighting against people who don't want to take risks."

There was an even bigger snarl on his face. His whole mannerism stiffened: his way of talking, his way of moving his hands.

I really wished Clara wasn't sticking to us like glue.

"What kind of risks do they take at a premium company?"

"Well, they were looking ahead eighteen months, and the inevitable premium is a Disney movie. I actually had the idea that Olympic mascots had never been exploited, and they ran with it. Amazing mock-ups. There was some enthusiasm, but eventually the executives at Burger Man knocked it back."

I liked my internship, and I liked the people I worked for. People sell pizza, and people sell shoes. Did he hate the entire capitalistic world? That's a lot of hatred for one guy. I kept my thoughts to myself, of course.

"Good for you and your exploitative skills," he said *out loud*.

Clara blinked at that comment. I could tell something was going on inside her head, because a different look came over her face and she seemed almost protective.

One of the new dance songs of the year came on. I never know the names of dance songs, but I knew I liked that one. I've always liked alternative sounds, but I've also always had a weakness for those forget-about-it-tomorrow catchy tunes with generic backing singers. I did not permit myself to think about my sudden romance being all over. I was desperate to salvage the great vibe we had going into the dance.

"We can leave the debate for later. Do you want to dance?" I almost pleaded.

Vaughan scrunched his nose. "To this?"

I had a horrible fact to admit to myself: I no longer liked the God of Room 207 very much. Jeremy and Paulette had figured out how horrible he was before me, but the reality of how much the person I was involved with was just a good-looking jerk hit me over the head like a hammer.

"You don't have to dance with me after all," I said sharply. "We can just stand here knocking my life."

"Hey, calm down," Vaughan said, and leaned closer to Clara to ask her something.

But instead of answering him, she followed me as I walked to the bathroom.

I started crying, and she spotted the first tears right away like best friends do. "We have to stop keeping secrets," she said sympathetically. And then she gave me a big squeeze, her outfit muffling my sniffles. "Personally, I think you have no idea how much you're worth. Or who you're worth attracting."

When we returned to the dance floor, Blanca was making out with Jeremy. Willie was dancing too, with a girl whose face I couldn't discern. (Although, I could tell by her silver helmet and horns that she was supposed to be a Viking girl.)

Clara got asked to dance almost immediately by Mark Bruin, from the math team.

"No, thank you," she said, although she looked conflicted.

Lately I had heard her mentioning his name more frequently, ever since he had ranked me on the stairwell. By the look in his eye, he ranked her near Tara. Had she really told me everything from that afternoon? I needed to get myself together. "Go dance with him," I whispered. And she did.

I breathed out when I was alone, and I found myself looking for Zane. I spotted him sitting with shy Sara Schwartz on the gym bleachers. Had he asked her to the dance, or had they come as two birds of a feather, two bashful souls? All I knew was that they looked pretty happy talking to each other.

I walked over near them. Sara looked flabbergasted when I said to him, "Can I talk to you for a second?" My voice was shaky.

"What is it?" Zane said incredulously, and then snuck a look at Sara.

"Can I have a tiny second of privacy?"

He stood and walked me a few feet away. "What?"

"I made a mistake. You're not pathetic. I'm the pathetic one for not seeing more clearly how nice you are." I accidentally hit him in the head with a spider limb when I said that.

"Oh, are you?"

I wasn't sure what I expected him to say, but certainly not *that*. "I—I didn't mean to be condescending," I stammered.

Zane just looked at me and said, "I'm here with Sara now. Let's discuss this another time, okay?"

A slow song came on. I didn't know where to go next. Almost instinctively, I headed back to Vaughan, who was dancing with one of the senior girls.

"We're just friends," she said when she spotted me.

"I'm going now," I said to my "date" after reaching up and tapping him on his shoulder.

I realized I had absolutely nothing else suitable to say to him. In fact, I had nothing to say to him at all. I turned and walked away. I looked around.

Clara was making out with Mark. Perhaps I really deserved this terrible fate since I hadn't been much of a friend to anyone.

209

* * *

Outside the door of my school there were a lot of pebbles that had somehow made their way onto the sidewalk from the gravel around the big oak tree.

I kicked a big muddied one really far.

I hailed a cab cruising down the avenue. I knew it was expensive, but I decided I needed to spend the money to get home.

When I staggered inside my door, my parents were in the middle of a Scrabble game.

They took one look at my face, and there were all sorts of empathetic sounds coming out of their mouths.

"I can't go to school on Monday," I said at the end of my woeful tale. "Everyone is going to think I'm such a loser."

Mom gasped. "Nonsense. You're a national essay contest winner. Everyone in school must be so impressed with you."

"Vaughan is in my precalculus class, and Zane is in both."

My dad looked at my mother. "Zane? Who's Zane?"

"He asked me to the dance after Vaughan. He's the really nice one, and I turned him down. He was there with someone else and wanted nothing to do with me. But there was this stupid notebook issue between us—" I couldn't continue because I had begun to sob.

My mother stroked my hair. "Notebook what?"

I wouldn't elaborate.

My sister called me from Princeton on her cell. I was sure when Dad went to the bathroom he'd called and told her to call me, but still, I was happy to hear from her, as I knew she would be more attuned to high school humiliation.

She never even mentioned Vaughan. She started in with "I never told you the full story about how Greg and I broke up."

Greg was her Columbia grad student guy, whose age appalled Dad.

"Men can be pigs," she said.

At the word *pigs*, I laughed for the first time of the night and told her what Vaughan's costume said.

She went hysterical on the other end of the line.

"So, how's school?" I managed, so I wouldn't be 100 percent self-centered, something she is always accusing me of.

"Good. I've been changing my research focus again."

"Wasn't it something to do with fish lighting up?" I asked.

"Luminosity of the laterneye—yeah, that was my old idea. I don't actually remember telling you about that."

"Mom did. Anything you do, she is over the moon."

"She is pretty over the moon about your essay award—"

"There's a first for anything." I tried to make that come out funny, but instead it came out a little too bittersweet.

"Funny you should mention Mom. She has something to do with my new research."

"Have you gathered one hundred science-obsessed mothers in a room somewhere?"

"No, I'm thinking of doing my research on neurodiversity."

"Whatever that is."

"What it means is that while environment is important, genetics is even more important. Some people are born with a visual-spatial brain—like Mom and me. We see things in pictures."

"What does that mean? Don't we all?"

"Well, you know how you and Dad are always telling stories, always have a way with words, and you're very social people? That's a different brain style altogether. I'm guessing you think in words. That's what the literature says regarding people like you."

"I'm your sister, Sari. You're talking like a robot to me."

She laughed. "Sorry. Visual-spatial thinkers are usually more uncomfortable with people. More awkward, like Mom and me."

"I think I understand. . . ."

212

"It gets more interesting, though, because no one is exactly the same. That's why even though we have the same parents, we have different ingredients in our own mix. Everyone is like a genetic stew of their ancestors, except some of us get more carrots, and some of us get more string beans."

"But no onions, I hope. I hate onions."

She ignored my wisecrack and kept talking. "But even if you think in words, you have to have some of Mom's brain style in you. Manhattan Science classes are tough, and, well, what was your last math test score?"

"Eighty in precalculus."

"Eighty is not terrible."

"Oh, such charity on your part."

"Just shut up, Jordie, will you? I'm trying to say that an eighty is holding your own in a school that is full of math geniuses. Plus you've gotten a hundred on almost every English exam you've ever taken. You should applaud yourself for your overall ability."

"You did very well in English, Miss I'm-Just-a-Visual-Spatial-Thinker."

"Fair enough. But I'm book smart when it comes to English. And I'm much more organized than you. I took good notes, and I always knew what the teacher wanted. But your writing always has more creativity. More risks. More energy. I only wish I could make people laugh or sigh the way you do with your writing. I can't even begin to explain how envious of your talent I am."

This was perhaps the single nicest thing my sister has ever said to me in my life. And I stopped myself from another sarcastic comment to say simply, "Thank you."

And her answer was just as direct: "You're welcome." 213

You could almost feel the sisterly love buzzing through the wireless network.

Finally, just to fill the silence, I said, "Okay, enough pep talk. I'm trying to get over a guy here."

"There's our girl," Dad said when I hung up and he saw I was much more at ease. "What did Sari say to you that we didn't think of?"

"We just had a little talk, that's all."

"It's amazing how you girls get along these days," Mom said.

"Considering how neurodiverse we are."

"Where did you even learn that word?" Mom asked.

"What's that supposed to mean?" I found the way she said that quite insulting.

"I meant that you don't seem to have an interest in—"

"I just heard it from your visual-spatial daughter. She thinks I think in words."

"Doesn't everyone?" Dad said. He turned to my mother. "Three words. Leave. It. Alone."

"I wasn't trying to—" Mom stopped her sentence with a troubled look on her face. "Do you think I treat you that much differently from your sister? I couldn't love you any more than I do—"

"Actually, I do, Mom."

"I understand her better. But I love you just as much."

"Let's change the topic," I said. "I can't handle this right now."

She rose to her feet. There were tears in her eyes as she went to the kitchen for a glass of water.

"Handle it," Dad said. "Your mother needs you as much as you need her."

"This was my crisis, not hers," I whispered.

He grabbed a pad and scribbled something. He yanked on my shirt so I would read what he wrote: *Give her a hug.*

I rolled my eyes at him. Mom is not especially huggable. In fact, I was sure that the last time I hugged her was freshman year.

He actually pushed me in her direction. "Mom?" I said when I reached the kitchen.

"Yes?"

"Can I give you a hug?"

Her face brightened considerably. "Of course, darling."

She embraced me tightly, and midsqueeze she started to weep. She was still holding on to me, though. I really felt her hurting, but this was such a rare event that I had no idea what to say or do for her.

"I don't ever like to see my little girl hurt," she whispered in my ear when she calmed a little.

When eventually she let go, I kissed her on the cheek.

Now Mom decided to make the three of us chamomile tea. As the kettle was heating, I was so glad I had my parents together.

"We're having a pajama party," Mom announced, and then disappeared. Truly, we *were* having a pajama party. When she returned she threw me a pair of red and orange striped ones I had never seen before. "I was going to give everyone a pair of Dr. Dentons for Hannukah." She held on to a pair of pink and green ones.

Dad held up his pair, which had navy and green stripes, and grinned.

Our Dr. Dentons had tush panels so you could go to the bathroom without having to take the whole rigmarole off. It was especially hilarious to see my mom wearing them when she returned from the bathroom pretending to suck her thumb. I was used to my father's shenanigans, but now I was sure that my mother had a sense of humor too.

But then she leaned over to me and wiped a bit of "dirt" off my cheek with a wet finger. I was a little afraid that Mom had lost it, and that she was next going to serve us some jelly sandwiches cut into cutesy shapes with cookie cutters. (That's how she taught Sari and me what a trapezoid and a hexagon were at the age of two.) But despite the ridiculous sight of three-quarters of my family in tushy-paneled Dr. Dentons, we soon went back to talking about our peculiar family dynamic and how we could work things out better.

That night I slept right in the middle of my parents in my footsies. I could see why Vaughan's sister felt so safe when she did that. The world was a scary place.

16. Measure Your Success

Even if you succeed, you must measure
the success and focus on how you did it—
there's still something new to learn.
Every good marketing pro does this.
It's never over, because some new
brand is always out there trying to
get market share.

On Sunday there was not even a phone call from the creep.

I was ready to call him, but each time, I pulled back my hand. I didn't want him back, did I? I had my pride, at least.

Clara called me first. She meant to be comforting, but after the dance she had a new boyfriend, Mark, and her joy over this leaked though. She sensed she better get off the phone.

Willie checked in and pointedly did not mention his sister smooching with Jeremy, who, as it happened, called next.

"Clara told me all about it. Now, finally, you girls see what I see. Vaughan Nussman is an ass. I want to kill him—"

"How's Blanca, by the way?" I was tired of the whole topic.

"We're really happy," he said guiltily. "I don't know why I never pursued her before."

"It's not like she wasn't giving you signals. But you were stuck on Tara the Poor Model."

"Careful, I'm giving you sympathy here. Zane was giving you signals too, you know, but you chose a man who laughed at your humiliation."

"Zane hates me," I said.

"He didn't."

"Well, he does now."

"I'm not sure what to say about that," he said in such a glum way that I felt he knew something more than I did about the situation.

Monday morning I kept to my prebreakup routine and headed for Out of the Box. I dreaded going there almost as much as going to school because I knew my supervisors would want to grill me on every detail of the dance.

"Ooh, is there big news," Brad said when I walked in.

"I don't think I can take any more big news," I muttered to myself.

"Sit, sit," Joel said when I walked in the premiums room.

Definitely, something was up. At least nobody was asking me about the Halloween dance.

"Don't tell me—they went and dropped the *Eggcups* idea too. . . ."

Marcus looked at Paulette. "You tell her."

"Tell me what?"

She didn't answer me right away, but simply smiled wide enough that I noticed her teeth had been professionally whitened. I was miserable, but it still occurred to me that

Paulette looked—well, really pulled together. In addition to her prettied teeth, she had on a red silk blouse and her hair was pulled back with a Chinese "sewing needle" accessory. She was wearing sleek pants again and stylish heels. Her face looked worry free too. Everything was working for her.

I tried again. "What?"

"Jordie! We're getting hitched!"

I leaped up to kiss both of them. For a moment I could forget about my pitiful self. "When? Where? *How* did this happen?"

"Well, I'm not sure you would have picked up on this, but Paulette and I dated a while back."

"Not sure she would have noticed?" Joel said.

Just then the big bearded boss they were always deriding as the Pope of Mope popped his head in. In my entire time there, I'd only ever seen him once. "You two are getting married? I need an oxygen tent. When do I get the invitation?"

A hush came over the room.

"We're having a small party," Paulette said apologetically.

"Of five hundred," Marcus said when the enemy had left.

"Talk about *cajones*," Joel tsked.

Marcus turned to me. "You are bringing Vaughan. This will be the party of the year. We're renting a loft and re-creating the old Horn and Hardart Automat."

"She's sixteen," Joel put in. "Does she even know what an Automat is?"

"I've seen pictures," I said.

"So what is it?" Joel challenged.

"It was a restaurant during the Depression where people put coins in slots and got exactly what they wanted out of little glass cubicles?"

"You got it," said Joel, beaming. "Just testing. We're going with a thirties theme. It's going to knock you out!"

"Joel's our enthusiastic designer," Marcus said.

"A nice change from premiums," Joel said to me.

Paulette cut in with "And there's going to be great thirties music too—and one or two B-52's songs from the eighties and nineties thrown in too—"

"Just a bit," Marcus said firmly. "I think 'Rock Lobster' and 'Love Shack' are enough. . . ."

Paulette's bottom lip curled.

"What?" Marcus said.

"No 'Roam'?"

"How's that song go?" I asked innocently enough.

"Roam if you want to, roam around the world . . . ," Joel sang.

"Okay, 'Roam' too," Marcus conceded.

"Thank you," Paulette said.

"This all sounds amazing, but can I quickly just say—I'm not going to have a date to bring. I'm over Vaughan," I interjected.

"What?" said Marcus.

"What?" said Paulette.

"What?" said Joel.

"What?" said Brad.

"I'm closing the Boyfriend Account."

I refused to tell them more.

My life was my own again.

"Well, you can bring whomever you like," Marcus said finally, when it was clear he wasn't getting any details out of me.

"I appreciate that."

In the warmth of my school lobby, I braced myself for the nightmare ahead.

"Hi," I said coldly to Vaughan when I passed by his desk. He was eating a strawberry fruit roll. In the light of day, he now looked to me every inch a boy, which I guess technically he was.

When I sat down and clearly was ignoring him, he pulled my elbow and whispered harshly, "I don't know what your problem is. I didn't want to dance to a song, so you leave?"

"Is that all that you think my problem was?"

Jeremy, who later said he could hear every bit of the ugly conversation, walked up and stood over Vaughan angrily. "Will you be a man and keep your mouth shut until the two of you have some privacy?"

"Like you're a man. He who is still living out sports fantasies like a four-year-old."

Somebody snickered, but already a blush of hatred colored Jeremy's eyes. "You know what?"

"What?" Vaughan goaded.

I'd never seen Jeremy's nostrils flare before. "You're a

fool. When all your senior buddies graduate next year, you won't have anyone who wants to hang out with you."

"I highly doubt that."

Just that second Etchingham walked in.

"Everyone turn to Chapter Four in our textbooks . . . ," he said sternly.

If I could push thoughts of Vaughan and even Zane out of my brain for the rest of the semester, I could maybe make it through.

"I need to talk to you," Zane said after class. I was at my locker getting my coat. The last two classes of the day were cancelled for something to do with school plumbing repair, so we didn't have French.

"I'm sorry I barged in on you and Sara like that," I blurted out.

He paused and moved his jacket zipper up and down. "Please—let me get out what I want to say. Sara is my cousin. It wasn't a real date."

I looked at him. "Are you joking with me?"

"Are we not the two shiest people in the school? Do we not look a little bit alike? She didn't have a date either, so we figured we'd just go and hang out. Believe me, we are not a couple, but she'd have died if I'd left her stranded."

They looked more than a little bit alike. Their hair, their nose—the only things markedly different were their gender and height.

"So what are you saying?"

"I don't know. I guess, just that—" He turned purple again.

"This sounds crazy, but would you like to come to a wedding with me?"

"Why would we do that? You despise me for looking at your notebook, and I despise you for being—"

"For being what?"

"Not yourself."

"Well, then," I laughed uncomfortably. "So you don't want to go to the wedding?"

"I didn't say that."

"What are you saying?"

"I'm just trying to fish—I mean, I'm just trying to figure out what it is that you want from me. Am I another project for you? Can't get the name brand so you want the generic boyfriend?"

I didn't say anything at first. "Listen, could you walk to the park with me? Please?"

225

We sat on a park bench in awful silence. Who was supposed to talk first?

A mumbling man nearby drew deeply on his cigarette like he'd never heard of lung cancer, and then he spit on the sidewalk.

"Nice," Zane said sarcastically, and I laughed. That broke the ice.

"You're really confusing me here," I tried.

"I'm a teenage boy with raging emotions. This is what you get."

"That's a bit dramatic."

"Don't talk to me about dramatic. You wrote the book on that—oh, sorry for that choice of words."

"But listen, that's who I really am."

"When it's not contrived, that's who I really like."

We had a meaningful look.

"So, where were we?" I said.

"You hate me and I hate you, and you asked me to a wedding."

"Yeah," I said.

"So, why?"

"Because I think I made a mistake about you."

"Stop now if this is going to be very condescending."

"You know, your obnoxiousness right now is not helping me talk."

He smiled. "Okay, I'm sorry."

226

"Look, I'm a teenage girl with raging emotions, cut me some slack."

He laughed at that.

"I'm trying to say I think I really like you now, and that—"

"Whose wedding is it?" he asked. At this moment he suddenly wasn't blushing. As a matter of fact, his smile was stunning.

"My internship coordinators are getting married. They demanded I bring a date. They're very wacky, and the wedding should be a blast. They'll have a big jazz band re-creating an old Automat and—"

"May I expand on what I like about you?" he cut in.

"What?"

"Nothing that you had on the page."

"Can you lay off that for a second?"

He picked up my hand. "You forgot to market your spirit. To tell you the truth, it was doing its own campaigning all along, at least with me." He paused for a second, and added, "And maybe the low-cut shirt in precalculus helped a little too."

You've read all those fluffy novels where the gorgeous guy finally says to the lovestruck girl: "I like you just for who you are." That's just so fake. Because I don't care how smart and funny you are, if you're not taking care of your looks, you're not exactly going to be a guy magnet. And if you can think of a few good ways to draw some attention to yourself, so much the better.

My highly paid ad agency mentors only thought Vaughan was worth advertising for because he was the guy I'd expressed interest in.

But you know what? They didn't see Zane coming. And neither did I. You never know what will actually work on people. That's one of the weird things of marketing, that it is such an inexact science. Customer A is getting your message, but you pick up customer B too, and in the end that may be the one you want.

I already knew Zane had noticed me, and then even more so when I wore that push-up bra. *Everybody* noticed.

But finding someone who is great for you involves several different kinds of thinking. Creativity is wonderful, but so is good common sense.

If I had to boil it all down into one unified strategy: A *relationship is not like buying soap. It's just not.* It's worth thinking about what you're doing and who you like, but in the end—you must already know—it's best to be the improved you that you are.

To: All Concerned
From: The Creative Team
Re: Million-dollar Ad Campaign

Update: Rebrand Teenage Girl

1. Wipe the Slate Clean

2. Situation Analysis

3. Target Market

4. Create the Right Team

5. Improvisation—An Art Worth Learning

6. Allow for Human Error and Move Beyond It

7. Work with Surprises—Expect the Unexpected

8. Brainstorming: Make It a Way of Life

9. Take Risks

10. Sexiness Sells

BRAND X: *The Boyfriend Account*
is loosely based on Laurie Gwen Shapiro's
experience as a teenage intern in an ad-agency
madhouse, where, during downtime, the "creatives"
focused their sought-after branding skills
on her lackluster love life.

Shapiro is the author of three highly praised
novels for adults and codirected the documentary
Keep the River on Your Right, for which she received
an Independent Spirit Award at a televised award
ceremony from one of her favorite actors.
Unfortunately, in a state of shock, she forgot to
thank anybody, even her mother.

Laurie Gwen Shapiro lives in New York City,
her hometown, with her Australian
musician husband, Paul, and their
very musical daughter, Violet.